Life *in the* Balance

Life
in the
Balance

Jen Petro-Roy

Feiwel and Friends

New York

A Feiwel and Friends Book
An imprint of Macmillan Publishing Group, LLC
120 Broadway, New York, NY 10271

Our books may be purchased in bulk for promotional, educational, or business use.
Please contact your local bookseller or the Macmillan Corporate and Premium
Sales Department at (800) 221-7945 ext. 5442 or by email
at MacmillanSpecialMarkets@macmillan.com.

Library of Congress Cataloging-in-Publication Data is available.
ISBN 978-1-250-61973-0 (hardcover) / ISBN 978-1-250-61974-7 (ebook)

Book design by Liz Dresner
Feiwel and Friends logo designed by Filomena Tuosto

First edition, 2021
1 3 5 7 9 10 8 6 4 2
mackids.com

To Pam.
For never being perfect, right along with me.
For fighting a little differently every day.

One

The sharp *ping* of the bat echoes through the air to where I'm crouched in a ready position. Next to home plate, Libby Kemp, the best softball player in our grade—probably in the entire state—drops her bat and sprints toward first base.

I relax the teensiest bit when I see that the ball isn't heading in my direction, but I still stay alert. That's my job playing third base. Actually, that's my job as a part of this team. I have to keep my eye on the ball, whether I'm at bat or in the field. Especially when we're down two runs at the top of the last inning.

Get her, get her! I mutter under my breath. The hit was a ground ball to first base, and my best friend, Claudia, easily fields the ball and tags the base.

The stands immediately erupt into hoots and hollers. I hear Claudia's mom doing one of those whistles where she puts both her pointer fingers in her mouth and basically shatters the eardrums of everyone around her. I catch sight of Claudia's little brother, Jamie, doing his adorable victory dance—the one that looks more like something a chicken would do than anything that would come from a human being. And I imagine my mom up there, cheering and screaming along with everyone else.

There's no time for me to celebrate, though. No time for me to rest, either. Because after she makes that out, Claudia barely takes time to think before twisting around and whipping the ball across the softball diamond to third base.

That's where I'm standing, my mouth set, my glove held firmly in front of my chest. The ball barrels toward me, along with the second-base runner, forced by the player behind her to advance to third. It's all a matter of what's going to reach the base first.

In a movie, the camera would pan between the runner and the ball, then back again. It would zero in on the expression on my face and show everything else in slow motion—the dust floating through the air, the ice cream–truck guy dropping a Popsicle as he watches the ball zoom across the diamond . . . even the individual seams of the softball rotating in space.

In reality, I act on instinct.

Claudia throws and before I know it . . .

Thwack!

The ball lands neatly in my glove. Barely a millisecond later, I reach out and tag the runner.

"Yer out!" the third base umpire bellows. (The third

base umpire being Libby's dad, who sounds way too disappointed to be making a call for our team. Also, since he has a cold, his bellow sounds more like a frog with a megaphone.)

"Yes!" I pump my fist in the air and try to stifle the massive smile threatening to spread across my face. It's my first double play all year, but I don't want to be one of those braggy girls who go around saying how awesome they are at everything. Libby Kemp is like that. *Everyone* knows that she trained with the All-Star Travel Softball Team last year, because it's the only thing she's talked about since. Seriously. I complimented her on her haircut one day and she told me she'd *thought* about getting that specific haircut during the spring and summer she'd trained with the All-Star team.

"I wasn't old enough *officially*, but they still let me go to practices." Then Libby swished that new haircut over her shoulder. "It was *such* a relief to practice with older kids."

I join the rest of the team jogging toward the dugout and give Claudia a high five. "Nice work!"

She shakes her arm out, her face a mix of pain and exhilaration. "Thank God you caught that. I threw the ball so hard my shoulder almost fell off."

"I . . . don't think that's possible."

Claudia shoves me. "You know what I mean! But seriously, I think all that extra practice we've been doing with your mom is paying off." She points between me and her, then back again. "We've got a connection, Veronica."

I giggle. "You sound all woo-woo. Have you been getting psychic readings from your aunt again?"

"No. Well, once . . ." Claudia trails off. "She babysat me and Jamie the other night and I was so annoyed about Mom and Dad thinking I needed a babysitter in sixth grade that Aunt Nina gave me a reading. Usually she says I'm too young to 'access the grand powers of the universe' or whatever." She holds her hands up in air quotes.

"And she said . . . ?"

"That the future is looking bright and the people I love won't let me down." Claudia grabs my gloved hand and holds it in the air like I'm a champion boxer. "And see? You came through for me! For us!"

"I did." My heart is still pounding, but Claudia's fortune—or her "message from the universe"—makes my stomach drop a bit. It makes my eyes flick toward the stands for the billionth time in the past hour, even as my feet automatically lead me toward the dugout, where the rest of my team is waiting. I'm third in the batting order this last inning, and I know it's time to shift my focus. We have to score more than two runs to win the game.

But I can't stop myself from looking for her, even though I know, deep down, that she's not coming.

Again.

She promised she'd make it, though.

"Who are you looking for?" Claudia nudges me in the side as we settle down on the bench inside the dugout.

"Mom." The word pops out before I can help it. Usually, I'd make something up, like that I thought I saw a dog running by or a cute boy in the stands. (I'm not super into boys yet, but lately the mere mention of cuteness gets Claudia's attention.)

Claudia would probably have believed me, too. My voice would have been steady and convincing and I would have held eye contact for as long as necessary.

I'm good at sneaky stuff like that. I haven't always been, but you develop a skill when you've been practicing for months: The laughs, the smiles, and the excuses all get better and way more natural.

"Is she okay?" Claudia gets that squinty "Oh, you poor baby, what's wrong?" look, the one that Aunt Jessie gave me the time Mom totally ruined her Christmas party.

"Fine. Fine," I hurry to say. I feel like a rock climber who's accidentally lost her grip while doing something totally stupid. Something totally preventable. I need a safety harness for my mouth.

"Mom's totally fine. I mean, she practiced with us last night, right?" I think about the three of us after dinner in our backyard, Mom at one end of the yard with a bat while Claudia and I took turns fielding ground balls and fly balls and line drives. Mom was smiley last night. Mom was friendly last night. Mom was . . . herself last night. I bet it helped that even though it's only February, it's been in the sixties all week—perfect softball weather in Georgia!

I sneak a look at the bleachers again, then at the path leading to the parking lot. Maybe she had an emergency meeting at her law firm. Maybe *that's* what's going on— instead of Mom going out to a bar before coming home. Like the last time she didn't show up.

She promised, though.

She promised she wouldn't drink after work again.

"Yeah." Claudia shrugs, the "poor baby" look disappearing from her face. "Okay, cool. Just checking. You looked upset."

"Me? Nah." I wave my hands in the air so wildly I probably look like an orchestra conductor and put on my best "Who me? Nothing's wrong here" face. (Another thing I'm good at now.) "Mom's good. Just busy at work."

It's the truth. Just not the entire truth. (And maybe I'll manage to convince both Claudia *and* myself.)

"Claudia! You're up first!" Coach Robertson waves from his spot in front of the dugout and Claudia jumps to her feet, then grabs her favorite bat.

"Go get 'em." I give Claudia a thumbs-up and try to brush the dirt off my pants (which is basically an impossible task).

I should get ready, too—take a few practice swings and get my mind back in the game.

I can't help myself, though. I look back at the stands again, like there's a super-strength magnet pulling my eyes over there.

Of course Mom's not there. It's not like my fairy

godmother appeared and granted my wish in the past few seconds. Fairy godmothers can't change the past, anyway. They can't change the decisions people make.

Who people are.

Dad's still the only one there, sitting behind Claudia's parents and younger brother on the right side of the stands. I wave, but his face is buried in his phone. Even from my spot in this shadowy dugout, I can tell that Dad's upset. His forehead is furrowed, and he keeps shifting back and forth, like he has ants in his pants.

Or he's worried about something.

Or someone.

Dad finally looks up and waves, and I paste a smile on my face, even though my stomach feels full of bees and the smile keeps wibbling and wobbling at the edges.

Dad wears a matching fake smile. Anyone looking at us would see a loving father and daughter, connecting across the softball diamond.

"Good job, Veronica!" he mouths.

"Thanks!" I mouth back.

So at least he saw my double play. His phone wasn't more important than that. That's something, at least.

But it's not everything.

Because even though I'm glad my dad is here, and even though the ridiculous-looking neon orange hat he loves so much makes me groan *and* love him more at the same time, that bit of normalcy isn't enough.

Maybe I'm selfish to want both my parents here. I

know that not everyone on my team has two parents. I know that parents have lives. Parents have to work. Parents have to do all that important grown-up stuff.

Parents don't *have* to drink, though.

Like mine.

Like Mom.

Mom, who promised to be at my game tonight.

Mom, who I only imagined cheering for me earlier.

Mom, who broke her promise to me once again.

Two

When I was in fourth grade, Mom told me that it takes twenty-one days to make a habit. To break a habit, too. I had just run into the kitchen after school, sobbing that all the other girls in my class had formed something called the "Sparkle Club" and wouldn't let me join.

Tears mixed with snot on my face as I held my hands out to Mom.

"I can't wear nail polish!" I moaned. "So I'm not allowed to be a member!"

"Wait, what?" Mom put down the orange she was peeling and wiped her hands on her pants. I remember how the room smelled all citrusy. How Mom's eyes were so soft, focused right on me. "Why can't you wear nail polish? And what does that have to do with sparkles?"

"I bite my nails!" I waved my hands in her face again. "See?"

Mom looked. Not that she needed to. I had bitten my

nails for ages by then. Mom and Dad had tried all the tactics, too. They made me wear mittens during the day. They painted on that special polish that tasted all bitter and disgusting whenever it passed my lips. Mom even showed me some article about one girl who'd bitten her nails for so long that a massive nail ball formed in her stomach and got her sick.

(Now *that* was disgusting.)

I still couldn't stop, though. That's the thing about habits—you might *decide* to be super-duper vigilant, but then you start watching TV or paying attention to your teacher in class and all of a sudden your hands are in your mouth and five minutes later your nails have totally disappeared.

Abracadabra! Nails be gone!

Sparkle Club be gone, too.

I sobbed out the whole story to Mom. How Abby McMahon with her flippy hair and Camille Henderson with her flouncy walk had chosen a bunch of other girls from our grade to be in their club. How they all bought matching sparkly ballet flats and sparkly cat ear headbands. How they had to wear sparkly nail polish every day.

It was a requirement, Rule #3 in *The Sparkle Club Handbook*.

"Camille always wears *gold* glitter polish and Abby's nails are multicolored, each one a different color of the rainbow!" I imagined all the Sparkle Club girls having a sleepover together, eating pizza and making ice cream sundaes and painting each other's nails.

"Their nails are all long and perfect. But mine are stubby and gross. When Camille saw them, she laughed." I sniffled. "Abby said that polish would look dumb on me."

"Okay, okay." Mom rubbed her hand in small circles on my back. My breath caught in my throat, then slowed as I nestled into her hug. I was nine then, and even though some people probably would have said I was too old for hugs, I still snuggled into Mom whenever I was upset. At night, too, when we read chapters of Harry Potter to each other. I think part of me is afraid that hugs are like fairies—that once you stop believing in them, they'll be gone forever.

Mom finally pulled back and looked into my eyes. "You can wear nail polish whatever your nails look like, you know. No matter what a few mean girls say."

"I know." I just-in-time stopped myself from bringing my fingers to my mouth. "But wearing nail polish would just call attention to these . . . these . . . ugly nubs. It would make them look worse than they already do. Everyone would make fun of me even more."

Mom didn't assure me that *everyone* wouldn't make fun of me.

She didn't give me a lecture about mean girls and how awful they are. (Well, not a *long* lecture, at least.)

She didn't even try to convince me that my hands didn't look *that* awful.

Because Mom knew the truth: that in middle school, even a *few* kids making fun of you is the equivalent of the whole world falling apart. She also saw that my nails *did* look awful, all jagged and barely there. She could sense that, deep down, maybe I needed to figure out the solution for myself.

So instead, Mom told me about habits.

That our brain gets used to responding to situations in certain ways. That once habits are established, your response can become automatic. Which means that when I get nervous or bored, my brain tells me to bite my fingernails. So all of a sudden—BOOM!—my fingernails are in my mouth without me even *realizing* it.

Mom also told me that if I put in *effort* to change my behavior, to resist my brain's message and replace it with a new habit, then my brain could change the pathway it automatically goes down.

But it can take time, at least twenty-one days for most people.

So I tried.

I waited.

I tapped my pencil and twirled my hair and sat on my hands instead.

I bit my nails a whole bunch, but eventually the urge to gnaw on them wasn't as strong.

Eventually, I grew them out.

And as of this very day, I haven't bitten my fingernails in eight hundred and three days. That's a really long time. I've kept my nails grown out for more than two whole years.

I've grown in a lot of other ways, too.

I've grown more than three whole inches, almost as tall as Mom.

I've grown my hair halfway down my back.

I've worn all kinds of nail polish. I've done neon colors and sparkly polishes and even those cute little decals that look like paw prints.

I joined *and* quit the Sparkle Club. It turns out that Camille and Abby are super mean and I really *don't* want to be friends with them. (That's called *personal* growth.)

Not biting my nails was hard at first, but I managed to stop myself. Because I wanted to wear that nail polish more than I wanted to keep that old dumb habit.

I kept my fingers out of my mouth. I kept my nails strong. *I* was strong.

Could Mom be strong, too?

Three

I stomp into the house like I'm a little kid pretending to be a dinosaur. *STOMP STOMP STOMP!* I picture myself with massive legs and big dinosaur feet. I imagine the ground rumbling and the figurines lining the mantelpiece trembling.

I'm trembling, too.

When the other team made the last out of the game (after Amelia Underwood hit a triple to knock three runs in *and* Cara Dunbar got a home run), we all rushed onto the field to celebrate our victory.

"Six to three, baby!" Claudia made a "V for victory" sign with her arms as I gave Coach Robertson a high five.

"Good work, girls!" he exclaimed. "Victory dinner at Papa Luigi's? They have a special on Friday nights!"

My stomach rumbled thinking about Papa Luigi's famous pepperoni pizza, but I knew I had to ask Dad first before I agreed to anything. He'd mentioned something about "family game night" earlier in the week, which, as groan-tastic as that had sounded, seemed even worse now that I was mad at Mom.

If I bailed without telling Dad, though, *I'd* be the one *he* got mad at. (And mad parents have grounding powers. Kids . . . not so much.)

When I turned toward the stands, I expected to see Dad on his feet, cheering along with the rest of the crowd. I expected to see him halfway through the ridiculous victory dance he and Mom do when our team wins, the one where they bump their hips against each other, do a little twirl, and wave their hands in the air.

(I pretend to be embarrassed about it, but it really makes me feel warm inside.)

Except there was no one there to dance at all.

Dad was gone.

When I ran over to the stands, Claudia's mom told me that Dad had an emergency and she was going to drive me home.

"Do you know what's wrong?" My voice quavered, and I reached back to tighten my ponytail, as if by doing so, I was tightening my hold on my runaway life. "What kind of emergency?"

"I'm not sure." Mrs. Munichiello shook her head, then grabbed the huge tote bag that she lugged along everywhere, the one that shows she's an "always has it together" mom, the one she fills with snacks and water bottles and wipes and whatever random toy Jamie decides is his favorite that day. Today it was a bright yellow dump truck he was driving along the bleachers.

"Your dad should be home by the time we get there. I'm sure everything's fine."

Mrs. Munichiello's voice didn't sound fine, though. Her eyes didn't look fine, either. They had that narrow, squinty look, the one Dad has when he's trying to hide something from me.

The one he wore for weeks before my parents first told me about Mom and her "problem."

Was something *really* wrong with Mom today? A pit of fear opened up in my stomach, deeper than the ones I used to dig as a kid when I'd grab a plastic shovel and make plans to tunnel to the center of the earth. This pit felt like it was bottomless, like it couldn't be filled by anything except a return to the way things were last year.

I keep doing dinosaur stomps all the way to the kitchen, a mixture of anger and fear swirling together inside me and propelling me forward. I stop as I near the doorway, though. Because when I hear Mom's and Dad's voices, so soft and whispery, the anger part drains out of me.

That's one thing the history books never tell you—that dinosaurs get scared, too.

And, yeah, there may not have been a meteor approaching, threatening the extinction of my entire species, but when I see Mom and Dad sitting calmly at the kitchen table, Dad literally twiddling his thumbs, the entire situation sure *feels* catastrophic.

They're not yelling, like they have been for the past few weeks. The last few months, even. The sight of them side by side is so normal that I get angry again.

Because my parents aren't allowed to act normally. Not today. Not when Mom broke a promise and Dad totally abandoned me.

"You forgot about my game." The words drop from my mouth like they're rotten food I've tasted and spit out.

Mom's eyes quickly meet mine. Her face looks tired, and there are bags under her eyes even though I know she got plenty of sleep last night. She went to bed before me. "I know . . ." Her voice trails off.

I laugh bitterly, the sound surprising even me. I don't do anything bitterly. Any one of my friends would tell you that I'm a nice person. I volunteer to pass out papers in class. Last Christmas, while the adults in my family exchanged presents, I offered to watch my cousin Billy, who's basically a crawling poop factory.

"You forgot," I say again. I turn to Dad. "And you left. You missed seeing us win."

"I'm sorry, Veronica." Dad bites his lip, but he doesn't say anything else. I look between Mom and Dad, then back again. I was expecting them to make up a bunch of excuses about how they had to do important "adult stuff," or say that I'm overreacting.

Not silence.

I feel like dinosaur stomping so hard the walls will rumble.

"Do you even have anything to say for yourselves?" I feel like I'm the adult and they're the kids, like they threw handfuls of flour all over the kitchen and I'm staring at a mess I'll have to clean up all by myself.

STOMP STOMP STOMP.

More silence.

"You don't have an excuse?" I look at Mom again. "Did you 'lose track of time' with the other lawyers at the bar again? Did you forget to eat lunch, which made you 'extra tipsy'?" I flash air quotes again and again because I've heard it all before. Mom's been making excuses about her drinking for months now.

This is why I can't drive you to Claudia's house . . .

This is why I passed out on the couch in the middle of the afternoon . . .

This is why I didn't come home until two in the morning . . .

She always has a reason. Always has an excuse.

Until now.

Mom and Dad look at each other, then Mom opens her mouth. She closes it again, then lets out a soft sigh. "Honey, we need to talk. Something happened today."

My breath catches in my throat. "We need to talk," with all its drawn-out pauses and awkward silences, is never good news.

Good news is different. Good news gets blurted out excitedly, like when Mom and Dad took me to Disney World in third grade and Dad couldn't keep the secret for more than two hours.

Good news is shared smiles and dancing in place, not kitchens that feel like the curtains have been drawn tightly, expelling every bit of sunshine and light from the room.

"Your mom, uh . . ." Dad shifts back and forth in his seat. He's in the chair that creaks whenever someone moves, and that noise is all I can hear.

Creak. Creak. Creak.

It sounds like the footsteps I used to imagine hearing outside my room when I was a kid, when the wind moaned and the house settled. In my head, those creaks always meant that someone—something—bad was coming. It must mean the same thing today.

Creak. Creak. Creak.

"For goodness' sake, Dan, stop!" Mom shoots out her hand and blocks Dad from moving anymore. She rubs her forehead. "I can't stand that noise!"

"I can't stand *this*." I put my hands on my hips. "I'm going upstairs."

I turn around, ready to lug my gross-smelling softball bag from the hallway and slam my door behind me, but Mom grabs my arm. "Honey, wait."

"No!" I whirl around and pull away from her. "I don't need to listen to what you're going to say! I don't need to hear some apology for today or some promise you'll give me about the future." I blink back the tears that are forming in my eyes. Mom has seen me cry about a million times before, but I don't want her to see it today.

Right now *I* want to be the strong one.

"You have to hear this." Dad's voice is sharp, and I stop in my tracks, then slowly turn around.

"I don't *have* to hear anything." I know I'm being rude, but I can't help it. Why are parents always the ones in charge? They shouldn't be the authority of everything, especially when *they* behave badly sometimes, too.

Before I can stop myself, my mind flashes backward.

Mom stumbling in the house in the middle of dinner, apologizing for not being home in time to cook the birthday lasagna she'd promised, while Dad and I look up from our frozen dinners.

Doors banging and voices yelling from downstairs when I'm trying to go to sleep.

The tight grip of fear on my chest anytime Mom grabs the car keys and says she's going out for "just a bit."

"You'll want to hear this." Mom reaches out and covers my hand with hers, bringing me back to the table. Her hand is soft, the way it's always been. Some kids had a security blanket growing up. Until she was seven, Claudia toted around a little stuffed giraffe. She kept it in her backpack every day at school.

Not me. I had my mom. When I was scared or tired, I liked to hold her hand, to stroke the soft map of lines on her palm and feel her squeeze me back.

Her hand feels the same today, even though *she's* different.

Even though she's been different for at least a year now.

Ever since the drinking went from one glass of wine every few nights to way, way more.

Mom's mouth opens, then closes again, like she's lost her voice. I peer at her more closely. Is Mom drunk *now*? No, I don't think so. I do smell *something* on her breath, but she's not slurring her words. Her movements aren't all jerky, like they get sometimes. She looks tired, though. Super, super tired.

My heart hammers in my chest. Maybe something else is going on. Maybe the whole hand-holding thing is an act and they're actually getting a divorce. Are we going to move?

My mind spins out of control as I stare at my parents expectantly.

I don't know what they're going to say, but I can feel that my life is about to change.

Four

Dad is the first one to break. "Your mom got in trouble at work."

My breath *whoosh*es out of my chest. *Phew.* No moving. No illness. No divorce. Then I realize what Dad has just said.

"Wait, what?" I sit up straight. "What do you mean? Was she fired? Mom, did you lose your job?"

"No, nothing like that."

Dad gives her a *look*, and Mom coughs. "Okay, maybe *something* like that." Mom closes her eyes and rubs her forehead. "A client saw me . . . um . . ."

"What, Mom?" I'm losing patience with her. The barfy feeling in my stomach tells me I already know what she's going to say.

"I . . . well . . . I drank a bit too much during my lunch meeting. After I got back, I hadn't quite, um, gotten back to normal, and the client I was meeting with noticed what was going on. She, uh, told my boss."

Back to normal. The words echo in my head. Our family hasn't been normal for awhile now.

"You were drunk? At work?"

Mom squeezes her eyes shut. "I wasn't so much drunk as—"

I cut her off. "Mom, that's exactly what you were. Drunk." I spit the word at her like it's a gross spitball the boys on the bus think is sooooo funny. It's an ugly word, and it makes my mouth feel dirty. I imagine Mom stumbling around her office, talking about prosecution strategies and evidence and other lawyer stuff while slurring her words.

Now I squeeze my eyes shut. Clients shouldn't see Mom like that.

No one should.

Mom shouldn't be like that in the first place.

"What if you'd been driving?" I bite my lip as tears start to spring up behind my eyes. I don't know who I'm crying for—me or some hypothetical person who could have gotten hurt.

"I wasn't. I'd never do that, Veronica." Mom leans toward me, but I lean back. I can't lean away from reality, though. Mom was drunk at work today. "But you drank enough to get in trouble, right? That's still bad, Mom."

"Yes." Mom sighs. "My boss was walking by and saw it, too. She told me that I need to take some time off. To go to . . ." Mom's voice trails off, her mouth pursing like she ate a lemon.

"Your mother's going to rehab." Dad says, finally jumping into the conversation.

"Rehab?" The word feels sour in my mouth, too.

"I tried to explain my 'behavior.'" Mom uses air quotes, her lip curling up on one side. "But my boss smelled alcohol on my breath. She says I can't come back to work unless I finish a two-month stay."

The lemon face gets even more sour.

"Two months?" I realize that I'm repeating everything my parents are saying, but it feels like something has short-circuited in my brain. That I'm getting information, but nothing is processing the right way. How could this be happening to my mother? To *me*?

"I told her that I could stop," Mom says. "That I'm fine."

Dad snorts.

"I *can* be fine, I mean." Mom says "fine" again, even though that word has lost all meaning for me right now. Nothing about today is fine. "Fine" is a big fat lie.

Then I realize something. "What if you *had* gone to my game?" My eyes are wide with horror. "You would have been drunk in front of all my friends." I lean closer, trying to smell Mom again. "Are you drunk *now*?"

"No!" Mom practically yells, then jumps up and touches her pointer finger to her nose. "See? Perfect reflexes."

"Now, at least," Dad mutters.

"I'm just tired. But I'm okay. Really. I can't go away now." Mom's words come out fast and frantic. "I have another trial starting in a few weeks and I have to be here for it. I was just celebrating over lunch, anyway. We had one drink. Maybe two."

"I've heard that before, Annabelle." Dad's voice rises, but he presses his lips together when he notices the scared expression on my face. Not that I'm scared of *him*. I'm just scared of . . . everything.

He *has* heard it before, too. I remember listening to Mom and Dad argue from the hallway outside their room a few months ago. The words were muffled, but I could still hear hints of what they were saying. (What they were *yelling*, actually.)

Words like "I can change" and "I'll be different." Bitter exclamations of "I've heard that before" and "We can't go on like this."

I close my eyes, wishing I could disappear somewhere else, to a dimension where pressing "reset" on my family is possible.

"Daniel." Mom snaps at Dad and I take a sharp breath. Mom and Dad only use each other's full names when they're super mad at each other.

Dad's eyes dart to me, then back to Mom. "Veronica, we'll be right back." He beckons Mom to follow him out of the kitchen.

Mom trails Dad, her head hung low, then pulls the door shut behind them. I wait a second, then dash forward and press my ears against the crack. My parents may be smart enough to leave the room before fighting, but they're apparently not smart enough to realize that *of course* I'll eavesdrop on them.

"You don't celebrate by getting drunk at work," Dad snaps.

There's a pause, then some shuffling. "It was just a lunch. I was fine," Mom says.

"Rachel sure didn't think so when she called me to pick you up at work. How could you be so irresponsible? What if you had gotten behind the wheel?"

I wish I could see their expressions. Are they standing close to each other? Does Dad look angry? Is Mom crossing her arms? My heart beats faster with each word they say.

"I wouldn't do that!" Mom exclaims. "You know that, Dan."

"Do I? How many promises have you broken so far?" More silence. I bite my lip so hard I'm surprised I don't draw blood.

Mom starts sobbing, a soft sniffle that gets louder and louder. It drowns out the soft murmuring of Dad saying *something*. Is he comforting her? Telling her she's an awful person? Asking her why she *can't* stop drinking if it's hurting both of us—hurting *her*—so much?

A minute later, Mom and Dad come back into the kitchen, both of them wiping their eyes.

"I'm sorry for that, Veronica." Dad says. "And I'm sorry for leaving your game early." He glances at Mom, who's avoiding his eyes. "I had to get your mother and bring her home. I had to call the treatment center, too."

"Which you really don't need to do," Mom grumps.

Dad ignores her.

"Is Mom leaving *now*?" I ask him.

Dad shakes his head. "I left a message. The admissions office is closed right now. I'll call back in the morning, though. Your mother needs treatment as soon as possible." Dad sounds more serious than he did when my hands accidentally slipped off a softball bat and it flew into the side of his brand-new car. He sounds like a robot who's been programmed not to take no for an answer.

Mom doesn't meet his eyes. She twiddles her thumbs, then picks at her thumbnail. "I don't need to go."

Dad lets out a noise I've never heard before, a guttural groan mixed with a yelp. "Anna, please."

I look at the distance between my parents. I remember how I felt gazing at the empty bleachers. "Mom, please," I echo. I *want* to yell at her. I *want* to scream that she's been the worst mom in the whole universe. That she keeps letting me down.

I can't scream, though. I can't make a noise that loud come from my mouth. Not right now, when every part of me feels like it's shrinking. Even my voice comes out as a squeak.

"Mom, please," I say again. "Please make it better."

Please make our *family* better.

Mom finally looks at me. *Really* looks at me, like she's staring into my soul. Like all our protestations are finally more than just words. Then she lets out the biggest sigh in the universe. The galaxy, maybe. "Fine."

"Fine." Dad nods firmly.

I wonder if I'm supposed to say anything right now. I wish there was a script for me to follow. I just know that I can't say that *anything* is fine. My emotions are twisting and turning inside me like they're caught in a windstorm. I *want* Mom to go to rehab. I want her to get help.

I'm just sad that she *has* to.

That she's like this at all.

"But what if I miss you when you go?" I say the words automatically, even though Mom isn't home a whole lot anyway. She stays at the office late all the time. Ever since she started working toward making partner at her law firm, she hasn't exactly been around to tuck me in like she did when I was little.

Not that sixth graders *need* to be tucked in.

But just in case I *wanted* that to happen, she's usually gone.

And what about all the other stuff sixth graders need their mothers for? We just did a whole unit in health class about how important this time in our lives is. Mr. Maxwell called it the "Growing Up" unit, and it was basically the most embarrassing thing ever. He didn't separate the girls and the boys because he wanted to make sure kids questioning their gender would be comfortable. Which is really cool, but that also meant that Ryan Halpert kept asking all the girls if we had our periods.

No one answered him, of course, but it just reminded me that I *haven't* gotten my period yet. And now, if I do,

Mom won't be here to help me with all that . . . stuff. There's no way I can ask Dad to get me a pad! Or a tampon. Or know which one is better.

I grit my teeth, suddenly upset at myself for seeing Mom's good side. I'm supposed to be mad at her, after all.

"You may miss her, but she *has* to go." Dad says it quickly, like if he talks for too long, Mom might change her mind. "Right, Anna?" He takes Mom's hand and looks into her eyes.

A tear falls down Dad's face and I blink in surprise. I've only seen Dad cry once, when his dad, my grandpa, died last year. He sobbed by the graveside until his breath came out in hiccups.

Tears well up in my eyes, too, as I imagine Mom stumbling through work. As I think about her doing that for the rest of my life. My voice gets louder. "You have to stop, Mom. Why can't you stop?" I feel like shaking my fist at her—like shaking my fist at the sky. But all I do is raise my voice some more. "Just get better. Stop messing everything up."

Mom stares at me, her breath catching in her throat. She looks the way my friend Tabitha did the time she was pitching and I hit a softball right into her stomach. Then Mom straightens up and takes a deep breath. She blinks a bunch of times and presses her hands against the edge of the table like she's steadying herself. "Fine. I'll go."

"You'll go?" This time, a half-sob, half-hiccup from Dad.

"I'll go. Because . . ." Mom takes a deep breath. "Because I don't want to hurt you guys anymore. Because I have a drinking problem."

"Duh." The words flit out of my mouth before I can stop them. I think about what happened last week, when I needed help with my homework, but Mom had fallen asleep on the couch right after dinner. I can still smell the living room that night, the sharp scent of Mom's empty glass beside her.

Deep down, I know that even if Mom *doesn't* go to rehab, she'll be too drunk and distracted to help me with all that girlie stuff anyway.

"Veronica Elizabeth Conway!" Dad barks. "Apologize to your mother right now."

"Why?" I know that I'm acting like a total brat, but if now isn't the time to talk back to my parents, when is? *"You* were just yelling at her."

Dad grips his hands together so tightly that his knuckles turn white. He takes a deep breath. "You're right. I *was* yelling. I *am* upset. But your mother still deserves your respect." He sighs. "Although I'm not sure I believe that sometimes."

Mom winces, but Dad still gives me that stern "I'm your father so listen to me" glare. "Fine," I mutter. Apparently *fine* is the word of the day.

"No, Dan. It's okay." Mom gives him a sad smile. "Veronica deserves to be mad at me."

"I do?"

"You do." Mom uncrosses her legs, then crosses them again. "I'm mad at *myself*. For being like this. For being so resistant, too." She rubs her eyes. "It's going to be hard to stop and that's why I got so angry right now. But I guess that's why I have to go away for a bit. So I can stop *needing* to drink."

"You shouldn't *need* to drink." I say it the way Mom and Dad used to, when I was a kid and had a ten-minute tantrum about how much I neeeeeded that awesome new doll at the toy store, the one with the hair as long as Rapunzel's. They gave me the inevitable lecture about "wanting" things versus "needing" them.

I *needed* food and water.

I *needed* to go to school and learn my letters.

I *didn't need* more toys and games. *Or* to get my ears pierced.

Apparently Mom didn't learn her own lesson.

"You choose to drink. Just like you *chose* not to go to my softball game today." My voice rises in volume. Because if Mom says I can be mad at her . . . well, then I'm going to keep being mad.

"I know you guys told me this whole drinking thing isn't a choice, but it docsn't feel that way. See, watch." I walk over to the fridge and take out a water bottle, then twist open the cap and bring it to my mouth. "You can choose to drink or you can choose to not drink." I put the bottle on the counter before it reaches my lips, then twist the cap back on and put in back inside. Then I slam the door so hard that the fridge rocks back and forth. "Easy peasy. I made a decision. So did you. Except your decision means you have to leave me—I mean, us."

"That's not how it is, Veronica . . ." Mom stumbles upon her words, then presses her lips together and takes a deep breath. "Okay, you're right. I deserve that, even though it feels like a punch in the stomach."

I want to tell Mom that it feels like a punch in the chest when she forgets about me. When she messes up so much that she has to go away—from me—to get better. I can't find the words, though. It hurts too much to tell her how much I hurt. Instead I just point up at the wine bottles accusingly. Mom cringes.

"I messed up, Veronica." Mom looks at Dad, who gives her an encouraging smile. I give Dad a dirty look. Why is he acting like he's on her side now? *She* betrayed us. Dad should stay mad.

"You messed up a lot," I add, looking at the floor. My insides are tied up in a knot that even a Boy Scout couldn't untie. I don't know whether I want to punish Mom or hold her tight. To turn my back on her or beg her to stay.

"That's *why* your mom is going to rehab," Dad cuts in, as Mom sniffles and wipes her eyes. "Because she is sorry and wants to be here for us. Because she recognizes she has a problem and wants to change." He looks at her with a question in his eyes, like only her nod can make his statement true.

Not just because Rachel at work told her to, but because

of us, too . . . right? Neither Dad nor I can say that part, though. Because what if Mom denies it entirely? What if she's only *really* going because she's being forced to and this acceptance is just one big act?

What if Mom changes her mind again and says she's okay, like she's done before?

I don't know what I would do if that "what if" turned into "absolutely."

Mom nods back at Dad. "It's for at least eight weeks," she tells me. "At a facility not that far away, in Atlanta. You can visit," she says hopefully. "After awhile, at least."

I cross my arms over my chest. "I don't want to visit."

I don't think I can visit.

"Okay." Mom wipes her eyes again. "That's fine."

It's not fine! None of this is fine! The words bounce around in my head. We all should be celebrating my team's win right now, Mom there next to me as the coach of the team.

Except this year Mom got too busy at work to fit coaching into her schedule and asked Missy Robertson's dad if he could do it. She explained that she was under a lot of pressure trying to make partner at her law firm. She showed me her daily planner, filled with all her meetings. She said that she could still practice with me and Claudia, and that Mr. Robertson would be a great coach because he'd played baseball in college.

But Mom played *softball* in college. She almost made the Olympic team one year, which means she was *good*.

Way better than good. Her name is on a plaque in our high school, right under my grandma's name. Grandma Kathy was also a softball player.

This means that the game is in my genes. It's in my blood. And in Mom's.

Too bad there's another trait in there, too.

Five

"It's a disease."

Dad tries to explain things to me more the next morning.

"It's called alcoholism," Dad says. "It's a condition that makes it hard for Mom to stop drinking once she starts."

I've heard about alcoholism, of course. That famous actor that Claudia thinks is sooooo cute was in a movie about it last year. He moped around looking all tortured, sang a few songs, and pushed his greasy hair out of his eyes. Then, all of a sudden, he got better. His girlfriend told him he had a problem and that she loved him and *BAM!* he got better.

He got better because he chose to. That's what the movie made it seem like, at least. But Dad is saying something different—he's insisting that there's something inside Mom that makes it hard for her to stop drinking. That just like she was born with blue eyes and blond hair and a hatred for broccoli, she was also born with a gene that made her more likely to become an alcoholic. With a switch that got flicked on sometime after she had her first drink.

I hate that switch.

I wish I could flick it off, like the guy in the movie seemed to do.

That's another thing Dad says, though. That for most people, it's not that simple at all. That sometimes, the disease becomes more like a runaway train, with every drink adding to its speed. With every sip making the person want more.

That's where rehab comes in.

"So what's rehab all about anyway?" I cross my arms in front of my chest, staring down at my bowl of oatmeal. I put cinnamon and sugar on top, just the way I like it, but it looks like a bowl of mush this morning. "Why can't you get better here?"

My voice is raspy, probably because I spent half the night crying under my covers. I'm not going to hide it, though. I want Mom to see how she's affecting me.

I want her to feel as bad as I do.

"I guess I need space," Mom says slowly.

"From me?"

"Oh, honey, no. Not from you." Mom casts her eyes around wildly, like I'm a teacher and she's a student with no idea of the right answer. Tears shimmer in her eyes. I probably should feel bad for her—after all, parents are supposed to be strong. They're not supposed to cry in front of their kids. I can't let myself sympathize with Mom, though.

Then I'll start to cry, too.

"I guess I need to be on my own for this," Mom says. "To work on myself and figure out why it's so hard for me to stop drinking. I need time to be in my own head and to talk to people who are trained to help."

"Your mother will talk to a therapist and go to special groups," Dad pipes up. "She'll have people there who will understand her struggles."

Unlike us.

But I weirdly don't feel bad about being left out of the "Understanding Mom Club" today. After all, I don't *want* to understand struggles like this. I just want them gone.

"Those are the rules, anyway," Mom adds. "That we can't have visitors for the first month." Mom has a half-eaten bagel in her hand that I can't stop staring at. Do they have bagels at rehab? Comfy beds? Windows?

"There's something called Family Weekend after a bit, too," Mom says. "You can visit then. I'll be feeling better then. I promise." Mom scoots her chair closer to mine. I scoot mine away again. I don't want to hear about how Mom is going to get better and things will be so wonderful that we'll all dance upon rainbows on the backs of unicorns.

She hasn't gotten better *here* yet. For me. And that's what matters.

"I don't want to visit." A hurt look flits across Mom's face, but she covers it up quickly. But I still see it. It satisfies me, in the very best "I'm a mean daughter" kind of way.

"That's fair," Mom whispers.

I take a bite of my oatmeal and avoid Mom's eyes. It tastes as mushy as it looks.

Mom takes a bite of her bagel and stares around the kitchen. Her gaze flicks to the wine racks above the refrigerator. Or what were once wine racks, before Dad emptied them all out awhile back.

"Maybe I don't have to go," she says suddenly. "I already feel better this morning. I don't want a drink at all." Her voice sounds like mine did the time I tried to convince my parents that I didn't eat the last slice of leftover birthday cake.

I had chocolate all over my face at the time.

And right now, I can hear the naked longing in Mom's voice.

Of course she wants a drink.

She always wants a drink.

Way more than she wants me.

"You're going." Dad crosses his arms over his chest. I feel like doing the same. Why is she backing out of our deal? How could she *want* to?

"But—"

"You. Are. Going." His words are steel. Nothing Mom can say will break them. She must realize that, too, because she slumps in her chair and pushes her bagel to the side.

"I'm going," she whispers. "For eight weeks." She blinks. "But no more."

Dad sighs. "I'll take what I can get."

Maybe Dad will, but I won't. I'm still mad. I'll be mad forever.

And that's when I realize another thing Mom's alcoholism is ruining.

"Wait." I hold up a hand. "You'll be in rehab for eight weeks. Softball tryouts are in *three* weeks."

Mom grimaces. "Yes."

"The tryouts you said you'd help me prepare for." My face is frozen in shock.

Another grimace.

"The tryouts for the All-Star team that I've been waiting to be old enough for since I was basically born!"

"Yes, but it can't be helped . . ."

"The rehab facility has an open bed for your mother now," Dad interrupts. "The lady I spoke to on the phone this morning said that we're incredibly lucky there's a bed open. They're usually very busy this time of year."

"Right. Lucky." I glare at Dad. "I'm *so* lucky to have a mom who's an alcoholic."

Mom's face is pale, and she buries it in her hands. Her elbow jostles her plate, and her bagel drops to the floor, cream cheese side down. I know I've hurt her, but she's hurt me, too. I think about how happy I felt just yesterday as I raised my arms in triumph after completing that double play.

Victory seems far away right now.

Six

"It won't feel like that long." Dad claps one of his massive hands onto my shoulder, and I shrink away. "The time will go by before you know it." He waves his other hand through the air in a zooming motion, and I imagine it's a jet plane going at supersonic speed.

Whoosh! Time's up! Mom's home! Things are normal again!

I'm not sure if I know what normal is anymore, though. I look around the huge lobby that we're standing in and shuffle back and forth on the shiny floor. My beat-up sneakers look out of place on the black-and-silver tiles. My jeans and the TRAVEL THE WORLD: READ! t-shirt I won in last summer's reading contest feel like they're an insult to the huge potted plants and fancy picture frames surrounding me.

Then I look over at Mom's faded jeans held up by a belt, at her baggy college sweatshirt and slip-on clogs, and feel a bit better. Then I feel bad for feeling better. I don't want Mom to look all tired and exhausted like this. It's ten o'clock on a Saturday morning, which means that Mom *should* be at home right now. We should all be relaxing on the couch, watching some cheesy show on Netflix.

Then I shake my head, realizing what a fantasy world I'm living in. Because in reality, Mom would usually be at the office right now, trying to log more billable hours.

A glass of wine would be next to her, too.

The only place Mom *should* be is right here, in the lobby of Pine Knolls Rehab Center, waiting for someone to meet us and show us to her "living quarters," where she's going to stay for the next two months.

Alone.

Without her husband and her daughter.

Without her family.

"Two months is a long time," I mutter to Dad. Mom's a few steps ahead of us, so I figure it's okay to say something. As long as I don't let Mom hear that I'm going to miss her.

As long as I don't give her another excuse to try to back out.

Right before we left (before they *made* me leave to come with them), Dad pulled me aside and told me that we need to act happy today. That we need to reassure Mom that everything will be fine and that we'll be okay without her.

That we need to accept that this is our reality.

Yesterday, my reality was having to buy the watery

pasta at school lunch for three days in a row because Mom kept forgetting to make my lunch.

Annoying, but not awful.

Yesterday, my reality was how Camille Henderson, who sits behind me in science class, keeps trying to copy my answers during tests.

Irritating, but not awful. (As long as *I* don't get in trouble, too.)

Yesterday, my reality was worrying about whether I'll make the All-Star team and show everyone that I can be the third generation of Superstar Softball Conway Girls.

Super anxiety-producing, but not awful. Most of the time.

Today I have a different reality. The worst reality of all, especially since Dad keeps focusing on how hard this is for *Mom*.

Which, yeah, I'm sure it is. But what about me?

"We have to make things easy on her today," Dad told me right before we left, as I hovered outside his door. He'd told me I should "look nice" when we dropped Mom off, by which I thought he meant my jeans *without* the hole in the knee. Except Dad was standing in front of the mirror, putting on a tie while wearing his shiniest black shoes on his feet, the ones he never even wears on sales calls because they hurt his heels after a half hour.

Apparently today is important enough for blisters.

"We have to support your mother, so she doesn't feel more guilty than she already does." He pulled and twisted at the strip of fabric on his neck and it magically turned into a tie.

"She *should* feel guilty," I shot back. "She's the one who's leaving us." I flopped onto Mom and Dad's bed. Maybe if I couldn't see or hear anything then it'd be like this day wasn't really happening. I'd disappear into some alternate reality where moms didn't have problems like this, problems that were way more than the "problems" everyone referred to them as.

"Your mom has a problem with drinking."

"The people at Pine Knolls will help her with her problem."

"Lots of grown-ups have this problem. But lots of them get better, too."

People say that kids have big imaginations, but sometimes I think that grown-ups are the ones living in their own fantasy worlds.

A "problem" is when my favorite pink shirt is in the wash on school picture day and I have to wear my second favorite striped one instead.

A "problem" is how I have to stop doing Chorus Club this spring because All-Star practice will conflict with rehearsals.

A "problem" is something I have to solve on my math worksheets. It's exponents and negative numbers and "solve for x."

A problem has a definite answer.

Wash the shirt in time and you can wear it.

Decide to play softball because it's what you've always done. And because you love it, of course.

Subtract each side of the equation by two and divide by four so that x equals three.

A problem isn't anything where "lots" of grown-ups get better. Because what if Mom isn't one of those "lots"? What happens if she's in the other group, the one that people *don't* mention?

Do they become the negative numbers in their own equations, disappearing without a trace?

Now I look around at the lady walking through the lobby and wonder if she's one of the people who's going to fix Mom. Or is she a patient, one of the ones who will get better? I feel like I'm working out a tricky word problem in my head. If this lady recovers, will *my* mother stay sick? Do I need to balance this equation, too?

I glare at her, then look away, my face warm, when she looks back at me.

"Veronica. Smile." Dad nudges me in the side as Mom's lips twitch up into a small smile of her own, then quiver and collapse. Is she going to cry? If she cries, does that mean I can cry?

Or does that just mean that I have to be stronger?

I wish Dad had told me what to do beyond "supporting" Mom. Because I'm here. I got dressed, brushed my hair, and rode in the car. I walked through the doors of this place even.

I'm here.

But Mom's the only one who's staying.

"Ah, the Conway family!" Another woman, this one with gray-streaked hair twisted up in a fancy bun, strolls into the room so smoothly it's like she's on one of those moving sidewalks they have in the airport. Maybe she has those sneakers with the tiny rollerblades on the bottom. I sneak a peek down at her feet, but nope. Just shiny red high heels, the exact same color as her blazer and her necklace.

This lady is way too matchy.

"That's us!" Dad raises his hand in the air like he's a kid on the first day of school. "Present and accounted for!"

Dad is way too cheerful.

Next to me, Mom takes in a shuddering breath. I hesitate, then reach out and squeeze her hand. It feels normal, all soft and smooth. She has a small callus at the base of her ring finger in the spot her wedding ring rubs against.

Mom squeezes back, and I imagine that her squeeze is a language all its own. One squeeze means "I love you." Two squeezes mean "Now that we're here I realize that this whole thing is silly. I'm going to stop drinking and we can go back home and life can get back to normal."

I squeeze Mom's hand once, then hold my breath as I wait for her response.

All she does is squeeze back once more, then she lets go of my hand.

"I'm Annabelle Conway." Mom reaches back to tighten her ponytail, a gesture so familiar that my heart twinges in my chest. I'm not going to get to see Mom adjust her ponytail for another two months. At least.

Before this moment, I didn't stop to think that something so small would be so important to my life. I was worried about Mom not getting to help me with softball tryouts and how I'm going to explain this whole situation to my friends.

But she's also going to miss our Thursday movie nights. I'm going to miss the way she sings silly songs while cooking dinner and how she's the only one who buys the fun brands of cereal. She still did those things sometimes, even after she started drinking a lot.

Will Mom miss our movie nights, too? Or will she miss alcohol more?

I drop her hand.

"It's so lovely to meet you." The lady is wearing a name tag that says OLIVIA ITO, DIRECTOR OF ADMISSIONS. She shakes Mom's hand, then Dad's. When she reaches out to me, I notice her fingers, hovering in midair. She's wearing sparkly pink nail polish. It's not super sparkly, but it definitely has a shimmer to it.

Her nail polish makes me want to bite my nails again. It makes me want to stomp out of here, too. Why should this lady get to wear fancy nail polish and fancy shoes and even fancy dangly earrings when Mom's wearing her old Tufts University sweatshirt? When she's about to be locked up for who knows how long?

I glare at her fingers, stopping just before I stick my

tongue out at them. I still don't shake her hand, though, and after a few seconds, she pulls it back and gives me a polite nod.

I don't nod back.

"Well, if you have all your stuff, then you should say your goodbyes. We need to be making our way upstairs," Ms. Ito says. "The first few days are busy in so many ways and we want to make sure you get settled before . . ."

Her voice trails off, and my mind naturally jumps to finish the sentence.

. . . before you descend into the belly of this horrible beast of a building?

. . . before we strap you to some medieval torture machine?

. . . before we make you realize that you started drinking because you're unhappy with your family? That you really want to disappear forever, *not just for two months?*

I shove the last thought back into my brain, in the darkest, shadowiest corner, where I have a padlocked trunk especially prepared for it. I lock the trunk and cover it with a blanket. Then I throw away the key. I throw it as hard as I can and pretend it sinks to the bottom of the ocean, down where sharks and piranhas lurk. One of them will eat the key. Then they'll swim *farther* away.

That trunk will stay locked forever. It has to.

Dad is hugging Mom. It's the kind of hug I always gave my parents when I was a kid, when they used to put me to bed at night. I did it after baths and stories and tucking-in, before Mom or Dad went downstairs to do whatever adults do at night. (Back then, I thought they sat around looking at pictures of me and saying how adorable I was. Now I know they just watch television and eat ice cream.)

Before they'd shut the door, I'd give Mom and Dad what I called the "biggest hug in the universe." I'd wrap my arms around their torsos and squeeze as tightly as I could, so tightly that I imagined I was squeezing all the love out of them so it'd float down around us in a warm haze.

Then they'd hug me again and reassure me that no matter how hard I tried, I could never, ever squeeze them dry of their love for me.

I want to give one of those hugs to Mom right now. But as I approach her to say goodbye, my eyes are watering too hard to even see her clearly.

I don't want you to go.

Leave.

Please get better.

Stay.

The words aren't coming, though, even as Mom reaches out to me and squeezes my hand. "I love you, honey."

Mom's not arguing or making excuses anymore. But she doesn't make a move to come closer to me. She's acting like I'm a dog that may not be safe to approach.

I made her feel that way.

But she made *me* feel, too. And I'm not over that yet.

Mom hugs Dad instead. They embrace for probably a

full minute, which usually would be totally embarrassing. My friend Lauren's parents kiss a lot in public, which always makes us blush and avert our eyes.

This isn't so much embarrassing as sad. It's a hug filled with apologies and promises and missed memories. A hug that both is only for them and fills up the whole room with its energy.

Mom turns to me again before the director lady pulls her away to her room or her cell or wherever she'll be living. I don't care what they call it if it's not home. She wiggles her fingers at me one more time.

"I love you," I whisper softly as she disappears up the stairs.

Seven

A single star twinkles in the sky as I lie on my back high above the ground. Dad built this tree house for me when I was six, when I started getting really good at climbing the trees in our backyard. Most kids in our neighborhood pulled themselves up to the lowest branch, then stopped a few feet from the ground when they started getting nervous about falling and breaking their arm or leg or whatever.

Not me. I never stopped climbing, not until I reached the tip-top branch in the tree, the very last one that would hold my weight without bending and swaying like crazy.

Not until I could see the entire yard spread out before me.

I think Dad built the tree house so that I'd have somewhere I was forced to stop, so I could be contained within four walls without him worrying his hair off. (Unfortunately, that still happened a year later and now Dad is Baldy McBaldman.)

I don't mind being contained here, though. From where I am, on my back staring up at the sky through the jagged hole between two boards Dad didn't quite make flush, I feel as free as I did when I used to climb this tree to the tip-tip top. The night air is crisp, but the wind can't quite make its way inside to whip at my bare arms. I pull a purple fleece blanket over me anyway, the one I store in the special wooden chest Dad made for me to keep up here.

All my important "tree house stuff" is in the chest. Even though I don't have an annoying little brother like Claudia, I still like to store everything away where it's safe. You never know when a wild animal might climb up in here and make a total mess of everything. A raccoon got into our next-door neighbor's trash can one night and when I went out to the bus stop the next morning, there were coffee grounds and orange peels and even dirty diapers all over the street.

It was the grossest sight—and smell—ever.

That's why my chest has a combination lock on it. Because raccoons can't remember complicated numbers. *Or* open locks. I don't even think they have thumbs. So they can't get into my stash of special snacks—right now I have a bag of extra-cheesy popcorn and a bunch of those little fun-sized bags of M&Ms. (Which really aren't so much fun, since they only have about ten M&Ms in each. Sometimes I don't even get a red one, my favorite.)

The raccoons can't get in there and rip apart my books,

either. *Or* poop in the spare softball glove I keep up here. (My best glove always stays in my practice bag. Obviously.)

They can't get at the important stuff.

Tonight, though, all I want is my purple blanket. Tonight it's just me and the sky. Me and that single star twinkling above me. It could be part of a constellation— maybe it's the middle of Orion's belt and I can't quite see the other two stars that frame it. Maybe it's the brightest gem on Cassiopeia's crown.

It could even be the North Star, the one that Ms. Davidson told us in science class will always lead you home.

I wonder if Mom's looking at the same stars tonight. Ms. Davidson also told us that different constellations appear in the sky depending on where the viewer is in the world. Mom *should* have the same view as me—she's barely an hour away, not even in a different time zone or different hemisphere.

It feels like she's on the other side of the world, though; that she can't see the North Star—or whatever this star is—no matter which window she looks out of at her treatment center.

That there's no possibility she'll find her way home again.

I rock back and forth on the floor of the tree house, then stand up. Even with that glimpse of sky, the walls feel like they're closing in on me tonight. It's why I came outside in the first place—to escape from the trapped feeling inside my room—but it's even worse inside here. Is this what Mom feels like in her rehab place? Like there's air to breathe, but it's not fresh enough?

The sign over the door may have said PINE KNOLLS, but there are definitely more trees here at home.

I miss my mom.

The words flit through my mind, and I close my eyes against them. But that doesn't do anything to delete the thought from my brain. I just see them more clearly, lit up in bright colors against the darkness behind my eyelids.

"You're not supposed to miss your mom," I whisper to myself, even though I'm the only one up here. Someone could walk down the sidewalk below me. Or maybe the neighborhood raccoon has educated himself and can speak English now.

I still don't want anyone to hear me. If my words are soft and wispy, maybe they'll float away from me. Maybe they'll disappear, along with the feelings that have stuffed themselves inside my chest for the past few days.

"Why did you have to go away?"

I imagine the question twirling and tumbling over itself, then winding its way up into the clouds.

"Why couldn't you stay here for me?"

The words waft away on the breeze.

I can barely say the last question out loud. That's because I've worked hard to hide this thought from everyone else. It's a worry that makes me feel mean and selfish and uncaring. It's a worry that's all about me.

"What happens with my softball tryouts?" I know

it's not as important as Mom's health. As our "family as a whole" or whatever. But softball is still important to me. Mom and I have been talking about the All-Star team for *years*. It's why we've been training so hard, why I've been *working* so hard.

Now it's time for the payoff. The tryouts and the victory and then the schedule of three practices a week plus games throughout the state. While balancing it all with schoolwork.

Every time I think about it, my stomach feels all twisty and turny. With excitement, of course. A little nervousness, too, but that's normal. I'll get used to the busy schedule. I'm not even that bummed about having to stop Chorus Club.

Not really.

Because softball is important. As Mom and I say, softball is a part of us. It's who we are. So it's understandable that I'm upset that she won't be here for the big payoff.

For so much other stuff, too.

I picture the next few weeks at home without my mom. My mom, who promised she'd work on hitting with me. My mom, who told Claudia she'd help her with her batting stance. My mom, who used to be my coach and my friend and so many other things.

My mom, an alcoholic.

Eight

"Yesterday was the best day ever!" Claudia's voice enters the school before her, louder than everyone else in the general vicinity. As usual. I love my best friend, but sometimes I feel like I should invest in a lifetime supply of earplugs. If her intended career goal of becoming a marine biologist doesn't end up working out, she should definitely consider becoming one of those announcers at huge sporting events. She won't even need a microphone.

"Seriously!" Tabitha Young trails behind Claudia, her beaded earrings jingling around her face. "That place was amazing. Laser tag, indoor mini golf, batting cages, *and* go-carts? I never wanted to leave."

Lauren Gregory giggles, hiking her backpack up on her right shoulder. "I think the trampolines were the best. I can't believe I *finally* managed a backflip."

"I'm just psyched you didn't break your ankle doing one," Claudia adds. "That happened to my neighbor at a trampoline park once. He had to wear a cast for months."

Lauren shudders. "That would totally ruin my softball season. Maybe I'll stick with go-carts from now on. Even if Tabitha did kick our butts."

"Every time." Tabitha raises her hands in victory, and my friends all break into giggles, then high-five each other as I stand staring at them. It's been at least three minutes and none of them have noticed me yet. I look down at my outfit. I'm wearing a bright pink shirt with bright yellow flowers. And bright yellow leggings. I'm not exactly blending into the walls.

I cough and Claudia finally looks up.

"Veronica! Hey! Where were you on Saturday?"

A lightning bolt of panic strikes my stomach, sending every inch of the rest of me scuttling for cover. Does Claudia know we checked Mom in to Pine Knolls this weekend? Does she have some sort of best friend radar? Or maybe she planted a bug in our car?

Luckily, Claudia speaks up again before my mind has a chance to brew any more totally unlikely conspiracy theories. "I called you like a billion times to see if you wanted to come with us. I texted you a billion and one times. Where were you?"

Putting my mom behind bars.

Sitting by helplessly as my life changed forever.

Listening to music while drowning in my own tears.

Obviously I don't say any of that, though. I just pull my phone out of my pocket and look at it. The screen is black, so I press the power button.

Oh.

"My phone's dead."

"It's been dead for two days?" Tabitha pushes forward. "And you haven't charged it yet? What's wrong with you?"

Even in the midst of my angst, I still stifle a giggle. Of course it wouldn't occur to Tabitha that someone could forget about their phone for a single minute. Tabitha is basically attached to her phone. Sometimes I imagine an invisible cord tethering her thumbs to her phone screen. Even when it's in her pocket, or in her locker, where we're required to keep our phones during the school day, there's a still a connection. A bond, like the one I feel for my softball glove. When I put it on, it feels like home.

"I, um, was busy yesterday."

Technically, it's the truth.

"I went out with my family Saturday morning and left my phone at home. I must have forgotten to charge it yesterday."

That's also the truth. It just leaves out the part about how I left my phone at home because I didn't want to be reminded that there was a happy world out there going on without me. And how I forgot to charge it because I spent most of yesterday crying and trying to lose myself in a book.

"Whoops." I shrug my shoulders in a "what are you gonna do?" motion and hope that everyone accepts my answer. Which they should. Because I'm a very truthful person.

Usually.

"Weird." Tabitha pulls her own phone out of her pocket and clutches it tighter, like it's about to spring legs and skitter away. "You missed out on an awesome trip. We spent the *whole* day at that new entertainment complex. It was *epic*."

"Bummer." I *think* I'm making an innocent face, but Claudia still looks at me curiously. Did she hear something in my voice? She *is* my best friend, after all. And best friends have powers, almost as strong as that power parents have when they raise an eyebrow and basically know what the other one is thinking. Claudia and I aren't *that* good, but we're close. I can always tell when she's in a bad mood.

Maybe she can always tell when I'm lying.

I give her a reassuring smile and try to mentally send her the message that I'll tell her the truth later. Because I will. Absolutely. Best friends don't keep secrets this big from each other. She deserves to know the truth.

Just not now, when anyone could overhear.

Luckily, my friends don't seem to suspect that anything is wrong. Because a second later they all start gushing about their "best day ever" again.

"I wish you'd gotten my messages!" Claudia practically bounces on the toes of her sneakers. "We beat a group of super snobby girls at laser tag and then totally rocked the batting cages." She makes a swinging motion and practically knocks Ryan Halpert off his feet. I stifle a giggle as he gives her a dirty look.

"We wanted to get more practice before tryouts," Tabitha adds.

"Cool." I picture the three of them traipsing around the entertainment complex, faces flushed with joy and excitement. I hear the *ting* of the bat as it connects with the ball, and the *whir* and *whoosh* of the batting cage machine as it prepares to pop another ball toward the hitter. I can practically imagine being there myself.

Except I wasn't. Because I was with Mom.

"Sounds like fun," I add weakly. I turn toward my locker and slowly spin the combination code. *12 . . . 36 . . . 18.* It clicks open and I bury my head inside, preparing myself to tune out the rest of their gushing.

"It was!" Claudia says. Then her face falls. "Except I kept hitting foul tips. When I crank the speed up in the cage, I can never fully connect with the ball."

"You did fine!" Lauren nudges her in the side. "You had an off day."

"No." Claudia shakes her head stubbornly. "I need more practice." She looks at me again. "Veronica, is your mom still planning on helping us in the next few weeks?"

I twist around so fast that I whack my forehead on my locker door. "Aah!" My eyes water with pain as I clutch at my face.

Claudia leans closer. "Ouch! That looks like it hurts." She gently pries my fingers off. "Just a red mark, though. At least you're not bleeding."

So that's one thing I have going for me.

I'm not concerned about my forehead, though. Right now, I could be gushing blood all over the floor and I'd still be more worried about what Claudia just asked me.

A few months ago, Mom had promised to help the four of us get ready for the All-Star team tryouts. She said that since she couldn't coach our team this spring, it was the least she could do to work with us for some special skills training.

"We'll do some hitting and catching, and even a bunch of running drills." Mom had clapped her hands together, her eyes mischievous. "I'll work you girls so hard that you'll collapse on the ground. You'll be a bunch of exhausted All-Stars!"

Mom had promised us that in one of her sober moments, though, on a day when she hadn't had "one too many glasses of wine."

Mom had promised us that *before* she knew she was going to rehab.

I take a deep breath before answering and shoot Claudia an apologetic look out of the corner of my eye. *I'll tell you the truth later*, I mentally tell her. *Really.*

"Oh no!" I smack my forehead dramatically, then wince when I accidentally hit the spot I *just* injured. "That's the other reason I was busy yesterday. Mom left on a business trip. A long one. Like, for a few months." I make sure that I'm making eye contact with my friends. Apparently that's very important when you're lying. At least that's what I heard on a movie I watched once about secret agents.

"A few *months*?" Lauren's shoulders slump. "She can't help us at *all*?"

"She won't be here for tryouts," I say darkly. I think about dealing with the pressures of tryouts without Mom cheering me on. What if she's not here for all the games this spring and summer, too? I force a note of pep into my voice. "But that's okay. We can do it ourselves. We're awesome, right?"

I hold my breath as I wait to see how my friends will react. They seem to buy it. "What a bummer," Claudia says. "We'll have to send her a video of tryouts."

"I'd miss my mom tons if she went away for that long," Tabitha says. "You'll have to FaceTime her." Then she changes the subject, pulling out her phone (of course) to show us this "amazing" YouTube video before the bell rings and her phone has to disappear into the dungeon of her locker for the rest of the day.

And just like that, my mom—and this weekend—is forgotten.

By my friends, of course.

Me, though? I know for a fact that what's going on with Mom will hover around me for the rest of the day, haunting me like a ghost with unfinished business. I'll never forget.

I may never forgive, either.

Nine

"Aaaaand pencils down!" Ms. Beatty, my math teacher, claps her hands twice, then snaps her fingers three times. It's the special signal that we need to pay attention. Ms. Beatty says she does it because there are always different types of learners in her classroom. Some learn visually, some need more explanation, and some need to do things for themselves until they can grasp a concept.

She's really great at understanding things like that, which is why Ryan Halpert always gets to take tests in the front corner of the room, so he's not distracted staring at the other kids. It's why Kristy Liu got an extension on her homework all last week when she had a dance competition.

(It's also why Ms. Beatty probably would have given me extra time on the test if I'd told her I was a ball of distraction today.)

Except I didn't. Because if I did, she'd let her eyes

go all crinkly and ask me if I also wanted to talk to Mrs. Styles, the school counselor. That's what she'd probably be required to do as part of the "teacher code." That's the same code that also makes all the staff members put those cheesy posters on the walls of their classroom—like the one of the kitten hanging from a tree branch. Or the bright yellow one where the owl says I BELIEVE IN WHOOOO YOU ARE.

(Insert eye roll here.)

Except maybe I should have made up some excuse. Because while the rest of my classmates are putting down their pencils (or in Ryan's case, spinning it in his hands like he's a baton twirler), I'm still staring at number three on my quiz.

3. Calculate the slope of the line when x = 16 and y = 4.

I should know the answer to this. We've been studying this stuff for the past week. But right now all I can remember is that the slope of a line has something to do with its "rise" and its "run." But what does that mean? The only rising I want to do is out of this uncomfortable chair. The only running I want to do is out of this classroom and somehow back in time, back to last week, when things were different.

Back to last year, before Mom changed.

I'd also settle for running around the bases of a softball diamond. Because as much as I *am* stressed about tryouts and how much time the All-Star team will take up, I still love softball. The emotions twist together like a braid of hair, so similar, so distinct, and so utterly entangled.

"Ms. Conway?" Ms. Beatty is next to my desk now, her hand held out expectantly. "Your paper, please?"

I look at my paper again, the blank line after question number three taunting me. The blanks lines next to questions number four through twelve do the same. I have the sudden urge to throw my pencil across the room. Up to the ceiling, maybe. I wonder if its point would stick up there, like I've seen happen in TV shows.

I close my eyes and huff out a breath. I put my pencil down and give Ms. Beatty my barely-written-on quiz. My "earned an F for sure" quiz.

"Sorry," I say quietly.

Ms. Beatty arches one eyebrow questioningly but moves on to Claudia, who quickly gives up her test and leans toward me.

"That wasn't so bad!" she exclaims, wiping her forehead exaggeratedly. "I think I actually studied *too* much last night."

Thanks, Lady Brags-a-Lot. I press my lips together to keep the words inside. It's not Claudia's fault that I both forgot to study *and* couldn't concentrate during class. I don't have to be mean, too.

"How'd you do?" she whispers.

I shrug.

"Oh, good call." Claudia makes a zipping-her-lips motion. "We don't want to get in trouble for talking about the answers now." She nods authoritatively. "We'll recap later, at lunch."

"I don't want to talk about it at lunch!" These words *do* burst out of my mouth, this time with the force of a cannon. My eyes widen.

So do Claudia's. "Okaaaaay." She blinks a bunch of times and I wonder if she's about to cry. Did I hurt her feelings?

No. I didn't do anything wrong. She was being way too nosy. *Super* nosy. Who cares how I did on the quiz? It's not like one quiz matters. Not when there's so much other important stuff going on.

I should apologize, though. For the outburst, I mean. I'll explain the rest later.

"Sorry." I tap my pencil on my desk. "I didn't get much sleep last night."

"No problem." Claudia smiles, but while her lips tilt up, her eyes are still flat and tentative. She's wearing a mask.

Something I'm becoming way too familiar with.

Ten

Almost there! I dig my cleats in and put on one last burst of speed. I don't know what's going on behind me; I don't know where the ball is. All I know is that I just rounded third base and I'm getting closer to home plate by the millisecond.

Sometimes, that's all that runs come down to: a mere millisecond, the infinitesimal space between me diving for the base and the ball zooming through the air, nestling itself in my opponent's glove, and being brought closer . . . closer . . .

"Safe!" the umpire bellows, and I pop up off the ground and give a huge *whoop*.

Behind me, Lauren, who plays catcher, gives me a high five with her non-glove hand. "Sweet running!" She waves her mitt in the air, still with a softball poking out of it. "I was this close to tagging you out!"

"Nice catch!" I respond, even though I was too focused on my own sprint to notice what Lauren was doing. But that's part of being a good teammate: working to better yourself while also propping your teammate up. It's like the pillow forts I used to make when I was a kid: Unless all the sides are stable, the entire fort is going to collapse.

A team is the same way. And our team is *good*. Fun, too. Rec league only practices twice a week, with games every other week. Rec league is chill enough that I've been able to do Chorus Club for the entire first part of the school year. Singing is the first thing I've really loved since I picked up a glove when I was a kid. (*And* Ms. Gudelot, our music teacher, says that I'm good.)

"A voice like a songbird," she says.

(Ms. Gudelot was really sad when I told her last week that I was stopping. I was sad, too.)

Singing is way different than softball, but it's also similar in some ways. It's an individual effort, but you also have to meld with the larger group. Whenever I open my mouth, I have to be focused on the music—the notes, the tune, and my breath control. Just like when I'm on the field, where I have to keep my feet steady and my eyes on the ball.

Both singing and softball take my mind off the rest of my life.

I like that.

I head to the dugout and give my teammates high fives, then wave to Tabitha on second base, whose line drive sent me home. She gives me a thumbs-up, then crouches down, ready to run if Cara, up next, gets a hit.

I settle down on a bench to catch my breath. It's the end of practice, which is when we usually split the team up to play a mini-scrimmage. Even though I love the drills we do during practice, scrimmages (and games, of course!) are my favorite part of softball. True, throwing a ball back and forth with a teammate and fielding ground balls over and over again does make me better. But there's nothing like actually being in a game situation, feeling my muscles scream as I round the bases or concentrating on catching an incoming ball.

I started playing softball when I was seven, when Mom signed me up for the town spring league, bought me a miniature glove (not one of those pink girlie ones, either; I got a red one, my favorite color), and told me to have fun. By then, I knew that Mom had been a softball superstar. She kept all her trophies and ribbons in my parents' home office, on the highest shelf so I wouldn't take them down and decide to pretend they were castles and capes for my Barbies.

I knew Grandma Kathy had been great at softball, too. When I was nine, a year before she died, we went to a special ceremony that her college held honoring her and other student athletes. I remember looking up at the stage in awe, at the big plaque they'd given Grandma Kathy and all the people cheering for her. She looked so happy and so proud. It was the same way I felt when I played. So I kept playing. I started living the motto on my favorite t-shirt, the one that says EAT SLEEP SOFTBALL.

It turns out that t-shirt sayings don't tell the whole story, though. Because, yeah, I still love softball. Obviously. But people *know* I love softball. They know I'm good at it.

That means it's all they talk to me about (especially Mom, since it's one of the things we do together).

It means I'm the "softball girl."

It means I *have* to make every team I try out for. That I *have* to keep being good or everyone will be disappointed.

What would happen if I didn't make the team? If I *stopped* being that girl, the one who loves softball and only softball?

I don't know the answer to that. But at least for today, softball is still pure joy. Today, playing is distracting me.

Not in a bad way, though, like when I couldn't concentrate on my math quiz today. Instead, it's distracting me in an "I can't think about Mom when my top priority is to field this incoming ball" kind of way.

In a "focus on my batting stance so I don't strike out" kind of way.

In an "at least softball will be here for me when the rest of my life is falling apart" kind of way.

On first base, Claudia fields an easy ground ball and I cheer, even though she's on the opposite "team" right now. "Nice work!"

Claudia glances over and smiles, then gives me a thumbs-up. Phew! It looks like our disagreement from earlier is over. I'll talk to her after practice, tell her the truth, and we'll be better than ever.

I bet she'll even help me think of ways to make this whole rehab thing easier. Claudia's good like that. She may be loud and boisterous, but she's the most thoughtful person in the entire school. Last year when I was sick on my birthday, she came over my house, and even though she had to wear a mask and sit across the room, we still watched an entire season of *Friends* on Netflix. We still had fun.

(Even though that afternoon made me realize that it's really hard to laugh when your whole face is congested with snot.)

The bench creaks next to me and I look over to see Mr. Robertson settling down, his ever-present thermos of coffee in hand.

"Hey, Veronica." His voice is as deep as the bass guitar Dad used to play and still sometimes brings out at family get-togethers.

"Um. Hey." This is weird. Mr. Robertson is usually out on the field the entire practice, moving around and instructing us on what to do. He may not be *Mom*, but he turned out to be a good coach.

He tilts his head toward the bleachers, where a tall lady with bug-eyed sunglasses is sitting in the top row. "She was cheering when you reached home plate."

"Okaaaaay." I'm confused. I mean, I guess it's cool that someone's mom thought I did well, but was that worth coming over here for?

Mr. Robertson smiles. "You know who that is, don't you?"

I peer closer, then clap my hand to my mouth. "Is that Coach Ortiz?" My heart starts racing faster than it did when I ran down the baseline. With those big glasses on and her

70

hair down, I didn't recognize the coach of the All-Star team. "She was cheering for me?"

"Absolutely." Mr. Robertson pats me on the shoulder. "She looked impressed from where I was standing."

"Wow. I mean, um . . . cool." The words stumble out of my mouth like a toddler just learning to walk. "Thanks for, um, pointing her out." My mind flashes back to the rest of practice, to how I dropped two fly balls in a row and slipped in a patch of fresh mud during our warm-up run. All of a sudden, I feel like I'm going to barf. "Has she been here the whole time?"

Mr. Robertson shakes his head. "Nope. She arrived at the beginning of the scrimmage." He grins, as if he were reading my thoughts. "Don't worry, kid. You made a great impression."

Did I, though? I'm not sure what I'm supposed to do now. Should I wave? Wink? Flash a big toothy smile? Or should I pretend Coach Ortiz isn't even here, watching me and rating me and—I peer closer—is that a notebook? Is she writing *notes* about me?

I take a deep breath. It's no big deal if she's writing about me. No big deal if she decides to write a whole *novel* about my strengths and weaknesses and . . .

I shudder and force myself to look away from Coach Ortiz. Maybe it *is* a big deal. Whatever. I don't have to think about it, though. I just need to have fun.

But what if fun isn't what Coach Ortiz is looking for? What I have to do more than "have fun" to be a player she wants on her All-Star team?

My mind feels like it's going to explode. Why is everything so complicated lately?

"I look forward to hearing about how you do in tryouts."

I blink. For a second, I forgot that Mr. Robertson was there. When I meet his eyes, I freeze at the look on his face. It's the same look Ms. Ito gave me at Pine Knolls, the same one I imagine on the face of everyone I see now. It's pity and caring mixed up into one.

Does he know what's going on at home?

I look at Mr. Robertson closer, then jump up as his mouth begins to open.

"You should get back to the team!" I exclaim way too loudly. "We have more practice to do!"

Mr. Robertson looks down at his watch, then shakes his head, as if he's clearing out the cobwebs. "Actually, it's just about time to wrap up." He winds his way around the fence surrounding the dugout and yells to the rest of the team. "Good job today, girls! See you tomorrow!"

I breathe a sigh of relief as he walks away from me. Then a bigger sigh when I notice that Coach Ortiz is gone. A second later, Claudia bounds toward me, her pants, like mine, decorated with streaks of dirt. ("A softball player's best accessory," Mom always calls it.)

"Lauren and Tabitha want to go out for ice cream!" she exclaims. "Join us?" Her voice is more tentative than usual, like I *did* scare her off during math class earlier.

My first instinct is to say no. Now that I'm not focused on practice anymore, I keep thinking about Mom. What if

Mom has been doing so well at Pine Knolls that they dis-charged her this morning, while I was at school?

What if Mom *meant* it when she said she was going to change, and she worked so hard all weekend that she's wait-ing at home? She's sitting next to Dad on the couch, him complaining about some rude person on the other end of a sales call and her talking about how she never ever wants another drink.

Ever.

She *could* be there, like she's supposed to be.

Deep down, I know that's not true. I know that there's no happy fairy tale waiting for me at home. That fairy tales are filled with monsters and missing mothers anyway.

That's why my second instinct is to say yes. Because if I don't go home yet, that fake "happily ever after" can still exist in my mind. Until I see otherwise, Mom could be there, frolicking in a field with talking animals.

"Totally! I'd love to come." I sling an arm around Claudia and give her my best apologetic smile. "I'm sorry about earlier, too. Like I said, I was tired. But ice cream will defi-nitely wake me up." I make an exaggeratedly hyper face. "Sugar rush time!"

Then I run ahead of my best friend, toward the dirt path through the woods leading to the ice cream stand.

This afternoon is exactly what I needed. First practice, then my favorite dessert, followed by walking home with Claudia so I can tell her the truth.

Perfect.

Eleven

"That was, by far, the best ice cream sundae I've ever had in my life." I clutch my stomach and pretend I'm about to fall over. "I'm going to explode."

Claudia pokes me like I'm the Pillsbury Doughboy, but instead of giggling, I let out a moan. "Good thing you don't like cherries," she says. "That would have put you over the top. Also, I'm going to say it again—who doesn't like cherries? They're the best fruit ever."

I wrinkle my nose and shake my head. "No way. They taste way too sweet." I point my finger at her face. "*I'll* never understand how *you* like onions. They taste gross *and* they make you cry. Can't you see that nature is telling you to stay away?"

"Well, I guess I'm just a rebel." Claudia shakes her head and her long brown hair swishes around her shoulders. Claudia has the best hair ever, even though she complains all the time about how curly it is. I'd swap my straight, fine, limp, totally blah blond hair for her lion's mane any day. Last year, when my cousin Susanna got married, I spent almost an *hour* sitting in the hairdresser's chair, making small talk about the weather and my grades while she curled my hair. It looked totally cute. Until fifteen minutes later, when the curls came out and my hair was as straight as ever.

Not fair at all.

"Oh yeah, you're totally a rebel." I poke her back. "Miss Won't Answer a Question Without Raising Her Hand in Class."

"I don't want to get in trouble!" Claudia exclaims. "It's one of the class rules."

I nod authoritatively. "See? You're the *anti*-rebel."

"Fiiiiine." Claudia drags out the word, but she still gives me a silly smile. "You're my partner in crime, though. Well, anti-crime."

I smile back, but mine definitely isn't a silly one. Because even though Claudia *is* right that I'm a total rule follower (I never take even one *step* outside the "designated outdoor lunch zone" in the school courtyard), today I don't feel that way.

Today, when the girls invited me out for ice cream, I didn't text Dad to tell him where I was going, even though I *know* I'm supposed to.

Today, I figure it's okay to break the rules. After all, Mom has barely followed *any* family rules in the past year. If she can do it, then so can I.

I still stuff down a twinge of guilt at the thought of Dad sitting at home, waiting and worrying. Because I *know* that Mom hasn't come home early. I know my imagination is making up its own fairy tale.

I just have a *little* twinge of guilt, though, and there's so much other stuff hanging out in my brain that I can easily hide it. Like one more box in a dusty attic I'm trying to forget about.

I do need to take care of one of those boxes, though. I take a deep breath and turn toward Claudia, the words already forming in my mind: *So, remember how I told you that my mom was on a business trip? That's not actually what's going on . . .*

I open my mouth, but before I can say anything, Claudia starts talking.

"Hey, Veronica?"

"Yeah?" I'm still busy thinking of how I want to disclose the truth.

"Um, can we talk?"

"Sure, yeah." I wave at the cloudless blue sky above us and the playground on the other side of the street, the one where we met when we were three years old and our parents brought us to playgroup there. "We *are* talking."

"No, like I mean seriously talk."

"Oh." I slow to a stop, then turn to face Claudia. Does she already know what's going on? My stomach both drops and rises thinking about it, like my entire body is a roller coaster.

"Cool." Claudia has stopped, too. "So, ah . . ." Her voice trails off, and she tilts her head back to stare at that cloudless blue sky. "My mom and dad are separating."

She's still not meeting my eyes.

"They told us this morning," she says. "Me and Jamie, I mean. Over breakfast. I was eating my eggs like normal and BAM!" Claudia finally looks at me. There are tears in her eyes. "Dad's moving into a hotel room until he can find an apartment. Mom was crying when I left for school."

I reach out and grab her hand. I squeeze it hard, trying to send my best friend love through our clasped fingers.

"I don't know what to do." Claudia sniffles. "What if I did something to make them hate each other?" Her lips tremble, and even with her bright pink sneakers and beaded rainbow bracelet, my best friend looks muted, like she's a color picture morphed into black and white.

"You didn't do anything," I say softly, then reach out for a hug. "Do you want to talk about it?"

It's the question I wish Mom and Dad had asked me the other day, when they sat me down for my own life-altering news. I would have answered with a no, of course, but it would have been nice if they asked. Because sometimes, talking just makes things worse. Sometimes it helps to block out the world for awhile, to retreat into a cocoon of safety and spend a bit more time as a caterpillar.

Because as awesome as being a butterfly seems, change isn't always a good thing.

"Not now." Claudia shakes her head. "Can we just . . . walk? Maybe swing?" She points toward the playground, where two swings sit empty.

I smile. "Definitely!"

We walk over and sit down on the sun-warmed swings. Claudia doesn't need to know about my mom's troubles. That's too much stress for one person to deal with. Plus, Mom will be better soon anyway, so it's no big deal if I keep this little bit of information from Claudia.

I tilt my head back, kick my feet up, and gaze at the sky.

Then I fly into the cloudless world above me.

Twelve

"Dad?" I poke my head into the kitchen, but it's empty. No work stuff spread out on the table, no Ritz cracker crumb–covered plate left on the sink next to the counter. That's Dad's usual afternoon snack: crackers spread with creamy peanut butter. He says it was his favorite as a kid, and that he never outgrew it. Mom always complains that he never outgrew forgetting to put his plate in dishwasher, too.

The counter is clean, though, as wiped down and empty as it was when I left for school this morning. Dad's slippers are lined up next to the front door and all I can hear is the high school kid next door playing basketball.

I peek into the family room and Dad's office, but there's no one there. Mom and Dad's room is empty, too. It feels emptier than usual. While Dad's side of the bed is rumpled, the covers half pulled up and the pillow flattened with its usual head indentation, Mom's side of the bed is untouched. The pillow is plump and fluffy, the bedcovers so straight that I doubt Dad even rolled over in his sleep.

It's as if there's a neon sign hanging above the bed, blaring out an awful message: YOUR MOTHER DOES NOT SLEEP HERE ANYMORE.

I squeeze my eyes shut, then spin around and pull the door closed behind me.

"Dad?" I call again. Dad works from home selling some kind of special computer part, but he's usually done by now. Maybe he's doing yard work? I almost smile at the thought. Dad is not the get-down-in-the-dirt-and-work-with-his-hands kind of guy. Mom's the one with the green thumb. Whenever our neighbor Mrs. Thoren walks her dogs down our street, she always tells Mom that we have the best flowers in town.

I wonder what our garden will look like this year.

I head back into the kitchen and push all the thoughts of dying plants and wilting flowers out of my mind. That's when I see the piece of paper on the refrigerator, held up by the magnet shaped like a narwhal, my absolute favorite animal when I was a kid. (Now, too, actually. It's like a unicorn but real!)

Veronica—

I had to meet with someone. I'll hopefully be back before dinner, but you can make a peanut butter sandwich if I'm late.

Love, Dad

"Oh yay. Another peanut butter sandwich," I mutter. It's what we had for dinner last night. And what I had for lunch today. Usually Dad's pretty good about making dinner—he's a better cook than Mom—but he told me he wasn't in the mood last night. And this morning he realized he hadn't been to the supermarket in a few days.

Which basically means that I'm half peanut butter sandwich, half human girl right now.

It's already six thirty, but I'm definitely not hungry after that huge sundae. So there's no reason for me to be upset at Dad for being late. He's a grown adult. He's allowed to go places and meet people.

It's not like I'm afraid of being home alone, either.

I just . . . well, I'm mad he wasn't here to notice my little act of rebellion.

What kind of meeting is Dad at, anyway? Shouldn't he realize that this is a highly sensitive time and he should be here for his traumatized daughter? Not that I *am* traumatized, but what if I was? Who could be more important than me?

Unless . . .

I think back to the strict look on Ms. Ito's face when she told us that Mom couldn't have visitors for a whole month.

"This is of the utmost importance," she'd told us, her mouth all pinched, her eyes narrow. "Our patients need to separate themselves from their home environment. They need a break to concentrate on their healing and recovery. That means no phone calls, no emails, and no texts."

It felt like a tether had been connecting Dad and me to Mom, and Ms. Ito had snipped it with a pair of heavy-duty shears.

SNIP!

But what if Dad decided to go back there anyway? Without me? I clench my hands together so tightly that the blood drains from my fingers. How could he do that?

"It's not fair," I whisper.

"What's not fair?" Dad's voice makes me jump, and I whirl around, my heart pounding.

"You scared me!" Then I narrow my eyes. "Where were you?"

Dad blinks. "Out." He doesn't quite meet my eyes. "Didn't you read my note?"

"I did," I say slowly. "It said you had a meeting. Who was it with?" I lean back against the kitchen counter and pretend to be all casual, like his answer doesn't matter at all. Like him visiting Mom wouldn't be the biggest betrayal ever—well, besides Mom's.

"No one you know." Dad smiles, but it looks too big. Too bright, like someone turned the lights up too high.

"Okaaaaay." I realize that I'm tapping my fingers against the counter way too fast and force myself to stop. "Are you sure? I know a lot of people."

Dad grins. "I'm sure you do, honey." He places a hand on my shoulder. "Not this person, though. Don't worry." He walks over to the cabinet and pulls out his trusty box of Ritz crackers. "How was school today?"

"Fine." I watch Dad get out the jar of peanut butter, then a knife, a plate, and two napkins. (At least he knows he's too messy for just one.)

"Great!" Slowly and meticulously, Dad takes out eight crackers, one by one, then adds a thick layer of peanut butter to each. He arranges them on a plate, stuffs the napkins under his arm, and turns to face me. "I'm heading to my office for a bit."

"Oh." My mind whirls about for a way to keep him here longer. Maybe he was with Mom and maybe he wasn't. Maybe he really does care about my first few days without Mom but is afraid to ask. Maybe he doesn't care at all.

But all I know right now is that him walking away isn't what's going to help us. That maybe Mom is away, but at least *we're* here. At least we can (maybe) talk and laugh and have fun. Shine a little sunshine on the fog that's descended on our house.

"Hey, Dad?" He arches an eyebrow. "Can you play catch with me in the yard for a bit? Before work?"

"Oh, honey." Dad gestures in the direction of his office. "I have a bunch of calls to make. Let's do it this weekend, okay? Maybe you could practice for chorus now? You don't need me for that, right?"

The fog gets a bit heavier, and I let out a huge sigh. "Dad. I can't keep doing chorus this spring, remember? I mean, if I make the All-Star team."

Dad shakes his head like he's clearing out a bunch of cobwebs. "Oh, right. That's a bummer, huh?"

"Yup." I look at my feet. It *is* a bummer. It's why I haven't talked about it much with Dad or Mom. Or anyone else really. I really like chorus. I liked learning that I really *can* hit the high notes and that I am good enough to get a few solos. That softball isn't the only "thing" I am talented at.

It's my *main* "thing," though, and that's just the way it is. I'll get over it. I'll be okay.

"Well, then we'll practice later. Okay?" Dad doesn't wait for an answer before padding out of the kitchen and across the house. A few seconds later, I hear the office door click shut.

"Okay," I whisper to the empty kitchen, the only witnesses the open Ritz cracker box and a dirty knife.

Thirteen

When I wake up the next morning, it feels like my head is a cymbal and some overly enthusiastic drum player has taken all their aggression out on me.

"Arrgggh." I grimace and roll over in bed, pulling my pillow over my head. Even with my blinds down, the sun is still streaming through my window. I should ask Mom and Dad if we can invest in those blackout shades Tabitha has in her room. She's supersensitive to light *and* noise when she's falling asleep at night. It's why she's never been to one of our sleepovers. The first time she tried, Lauren's snoring kept her up all night.

(To be honest, Lauren's snoring would keep *anyone* up all night.)

I don't usually get headaches. Not like Dad, who complains a few times a month about his migraines. He has to hole up in his bedroom and shut off all the lights, a damp washcloth over his eyes. Even me whispering to him makes him clench his teeth in pain.

Dad once warned me that I could "age into" migraines, but I doubt that's what this is, even if the idea of a wet washcloth *does* sound good right about now. No, it's the nonstop crying I did last night that's making my head feel like one of those pictures of explosions in Lauren's favorite comic books.

After Dad retreated to his office and I had to squelch the desire to text Mom for advice on what to do if I see Coach Ortiz again, I could only manage about ten minutes of some random Netflix movie before I started crying.

(There's only so much of a "heartwarming mother-daughter relationship" storyline you can watch before you feel like the movie industry is directly targeting you.)

After a few minutes, I finally opened my eyes. I was still flopped on my stomach, so all I had was a direct view of my sheets, my favorite ones, light blue with softballs all over them.

"Live softball and dream softball, right?" Mom had said when we bought them, shaking her head in acceptance after I'd rejected the "oh so pretty" pink floral sheets she'd suggested.

(I am *not* a pink floral kind of girl.)

The memory of Mom made me cry even harder. Which means that this morning, in addition to my headache, my face is probably a splotchy mess.

At least the thought of getting out of the house makes me feel a bit better, even though it does absolutely nothing for my head. And Tylenol will help me there. I roll over and grab my phone from my nightstand, then practically shriek out loud when I see the time.

8:02!

The bus will be here in ten minutes! Why didn't Mom wake me—

Oh. Duh. The *Mom*-sized hole that had tunneled its way into our house gets a few inches deeper. This one is a *literal* Mom-sized hole. The figurative one has been here for awhile now.

Dad had to wake me up yesterday, after I'd pressed snooze on my alarm clock three times, then shut it off entirely. I'm not the best early riser, and both my parents know that. It's why even though I'm eleven years old, they still wake me up for school. It's why they tell me that now that I'm older, I need to "take responsibility" and "be more mature," but they still stomp their way into my bedroom every morning, allowing for just enough time for me to take a quick shower, get dressed, and grab a banana and a Nutri-Grain bar on my way out the door.

"If you wanted a proper breakfast, you'll get yourself up on time," Mom always says.

(*Said?*)

No, definitely *says*. It's not like Mom's dead or anything. She's just gone.

Temporarily away.

There's a word for that, those expressions that sound all fancy so you don't have to say the *really* awful thing.

Euphemism. It sounds like *euphonium,* an instrument my Aunt Kristen played in high school.

It also sounds like *euphoria,* a fancy word that means "really, really happy."

None of those euphemisms give me euphoria. Not at all.

Neither does being super-duper late for school. Anyway, I know *Mom's* not here, but why didn't Dad wake me up?

"Dad?" I shout it from my room, then again when I'm in my bathroom, a toothbrush dangling from my mouth. Good thing I took a shower before bed; I have no time for one today and I don't want to go to school as a total stinkasaurus.

I'm having a total flashback to last night, when I roamed the house looking for my missing dad. And after I throw on a pair of jeans (my too-tight, too-short, "whoops! everything else is in the laundry" ones) and a t-shirt, that flashback becomes a reality when I find another note on the refrigerator. Dad even pinned it up with the same magnet.

Veronica—

I had another meeting this morning. Have a great day!

Love, Dad

I narrow my eyes at the note, like there's another line hidden in there somewhere. Like if I put it under the lamp, I'll discover that Dad wrote something in lemon juice, like I used to do when I was a kid.

Like there's a logical explanation for all this secrecy.

And *"Have a great day?"* How can I have a great day when it's starting out like this? When I'm totally going to be late *and* my Dad's transformed into the Amazing Disappearing Man?

Dad never has sales meetings at this time. He can't be visiting Mom this early, either. What could be going on? I think back to Claudia's admission yesterday—are *my* parents going to get separated, too? Did Dad finally get fed up with Mom's drinking and decide to meet with a lawyer? Or what if *he's* at the doctor? What if *Dad's* sick in some way?

What's going on?

Fourteen

Luckily, I don't have much time to worry about Dad. Seeing the bus out your front window and having to sprint to catch it will do that to you. I'm huffing and puffing worse than the wolf in "The Three Little Pigs" by the time I settle into a seat.

(There's a reason I do softball instead of track, and the stitch in my side is exactly it.)

I've finally caught my breath by the time I meet up with Claudia in front of school. She's sitting on the stone bench outside the door, playing with the Apple Watch her parents got her for her birthday a few months ago. She was totally shocked when she opened her present—she'd begged for that watch for months and months, but we both knew her parents wouldn't get it for her. Claudia's parents usually got her things like socks and new notebooks for her birthday. Things that she *needed*, yeah, but boring practical stuff. Nothing as extravagant as an Apple Watch.

But now that I see it on her wrist, I wonder if there was a reason for that present. Like her parents were setting the scene for their upcoming separation. Buttering Claudia up so she wouldn't be so upset.

I scroll back across my own memories of the past few months. Did Mom and Dad do anything to cushion the blow of Mom going to rehab? My mind whirls, but of course there's nothing there. Because Mom's trip to rehab wasn't planned. It didn't happen because she realized she had a problem and wanted to get sober for me.

No, Mom's "trip" happened because she got caught by her boss. Because she had no choice. She's not on some exotic beach or taking pictures of the Eiffel Tower. She's in treatment. She's being treated.

"Veronica?" Claudia waves her hand by my face. I've stopped right in front of her at the door, lost in my own thoughts. "Are you okay? You didn't show up this morning."

"This morning?" I motion for Claudia to follow me inside. Mrs. Fink hates when we're late for class. "Were we supposed to do—"

I remember *just* as Claudia reminds me. "We were going to meet at the softball field, remember?" Claudia points at the softball field in the distance. "You said that since your mom couldn't do after-dinner practices with us now, we could meet up a few times in the morning?"

"Ugh." I shoot an apologetic glance back at Claudia, even as we both continue speed-walking to our lockers.

(Carefully, because Mrs. Hicks in the office is a total stickler for kids running in the halls.)

"I forgot," I continue. "I went to bed late last night, then didn't hear my alarm. Mom's away and Dad didn't wake me up." I pause for breath. "It was a whole mess."

My stomach grumbles and Claudia giggles. "It sounds like it. Literally!"

I laugh, glad that Claudia isn't mad. The last thing I want to do is to start letting down other people the way Mom did to me. "See? I haven't eaten anything all morning."

"I think I have a granola bar in here somewhere." Claudia opens her locker, then rummages around on the top shelf, finally emerging with a crumpled, ball-like object. "Um . . . well, it was a bar *once*. It's more of a . . . granola sphere now? It probably tastes the same, though," she quickly adds, as I raise my eyebrows dubiously.

"How long has that been in there?" I take the granola sphere and peer at the wrapper. "Do they even make this flavor anymore?"

"Hey!" Claudia puts her hands on her hips, but her mouth quirks upward. "I'll have you know that . . . wait . . ." Now she looks at the wrapper. "Oh no, I think you're right. They discontinued this flavor last fall. Ew!" She drops the sphere on the ground and we both burst out laughing.

Brrrrrrring!

"Ladies! Class." Our principal, Mr. Fredette, looms above us, his glasses slipping down his nose. We both jump, then simultaneously grab our Language Arts binders and bolt down the hall. Somehow, we make it through the doorway before the late bell rings, and as I turn to look at Claudia across the room, she holds her hand up for a long-distance high five just as Mrs. Fink pulls up a new slide on the Smart Board.

"I'll make it up to you later," I mouth, and Claudia nods.

She's smiling, like *of course* I won't let her down. Of course everything will get back to normal—to a new normal, maybe, but still nothing out of the ordinary.

How can I tell Claudia that she's totally wrong?

Fifteen

When I was in elementary school, we used to go to Cape Cod every summer, in a town where my Grandma Helen grew up. We'd fly to Boston, then drive the rest of the way. Even though the time in the car was way less than the time we'd just spent on an airplane, as a seven-, then eight-, then nine-year-old, those ninety minutes (sometimes longer if there was a backup at the Sagamore Bridge) seemed to drag on forever, like time was something measured in dog years. One human minute actually equaled seven travel minutes.

I'd sit in the backseat of our rental car, crossing and recrossing my legs when the seats got too hot and sticky. I can still feel the seat peeling and squelching away from my bare legs.

"How much longer?"

I was allowed to ask that question three times per trip. Mom and Dad had made that rule after our first trip to the Cape, when I asked for an update approximately every fifteen seconds. They decided that three times was reasonable—one question for the early flash of excitement, one question during the endless middle, and once when I could smell the salt water in the air.

I'd sing along to the radio at the top of my lungs, then curl up against the window and stare out at the other cars when Mom and Dad got fed up with me. I made up a game where I imagined a story for every face flashing by.

The elderly lady with the floppy straw hat was a retired Broadway actress traveling to her summer home, one of the mansions right on the water with wraparound porches and hydrangeas spotting the lawn.

The three fighting kids staring out the back window of the huge blue minivan were sick and tired of their parents dragging them around the country and just wanted to settle down, maybe in a little cottage by the sea.

The man in a business suit and tie, his hair slicked back like he'd already been in the ocean, was meeting his family at their vacation house after finishing up a long week of work, desperate to change into a bathing suit and feel the sand between his toes.

Everyone I saw was either going or leaving, stuck in that boring in-between place, where the fun either hasn't started or is starting to drain away.

"We'll get there when we get there," Mom would always say, then turn right back to her book. I usually tried to read in the car, but got carsick after about two minutes, while Mom could read practically an entire novel during our trip. "No sooner, no later."

Over the years, though, I started noticing the landmarks around me: the gas station at the rotary, where we always stopped so I could pee, and where I always convinced Dad to get me a blue raspberry slushy (the yummiest flavor).

The roadside diner where we'd stopped one year for a late lunch, and where Mom had left her favorite bracelet on the table, the one Dad had given her for their first anniversary. She'd cried for the entire rest of the drive after we went back and she realized it was gone.

Then the rock-filled driveway of the house we rented, the one with the weathered gray shutters and the bright pink roses lining the driveway. I always ran out of the car and buried my face in the flowers (watching out for thorns, of course—a cut-up face is no way to start a vacation!). For years, I thought those flowers bloomed just for me.

The rest of the week always felt the same way. It was filled with bumper boats and beach days, lazy mornings on the beach slathered in sunscreen, a pail in one hand and a shovel in the other. Mom and I searched for hermit crabs and shrieked as we jumped over the frigid waves, while Dad lay on his towel, his pale skin slathered in SPF 5000.

And every night before bed, we'd roast s'mores in the firepit behind our rental or walk to get double scoops of chocolate chip from Sundae School down the street, an old one-room schoolhouse that someone had converted into an ice cream parlor.

It's not the *fanciest* trip in the world, but it's still special, way better than the "epic summer vacation plans" Camille and Abby are gushing about in the lunch line ahead of me.

"I can't wait." Camille tosses her long red hair over her shoulder. I'm not even standing *that* close to her, and she still almost whips me in the face. Camille has the longest hair I've ever seen. It's Rapunzel-worthy. "We're going to Aruba for two weeks, then to California, where our second house is. You *have* to visit. There are two supercute boys who live right next door."

Abby *squee*s and claps her hands together. "That's amazing." She reaches for a fruit cup and settles it next to the chicken nuggets on her tray. "I totally *would* visit, but we're going to be away the whole summer. It takes a long time to travel all over Europe, you know."

I roll my eyes, just managing to stifle the groan that's actively trying to claw its way out of my mouth. *We know you're rich*, I want to exclaim. *You don't* have *to tell everyone all the time.*

They both *do* tell us, though. And the rest of us have been well aware of that fact since kindergarten, when Abby and Camille compared how many stuffed animals each of them owned during "sharing time" the first day of school.

I take a slice of pizza and a bottle of water (luckily I have some money left on my account, because there was no way I had time to make anything this morning), then head in the opposite direction from Abby and Camille, a heavy feeling weighing down my stomach even though it's totally empty.

It's not that I'm jealous of Abby's European tour or Camille's fancy second house. It's just that their conversation is like a slap in the face, the one totally random thing that made this whole "Mom's in rehab" thing seem one hundred percent, "going to affect the future" real.

Maybe I don't want to go to Europe, but I *do* want to go to Cape Cod. *Will* we still get to go on vacation this summer if Mom's in recovery? Dad told me that after Mom comes home, she's going to have to go to support groups and meetings all the time. She's going to have to meet with a therapist and keep a routine.

Are s'mores part of a routine?

I probably don't even need to ask Dad about our vacation plans. Mom's addiction will change *that*, just like it's changing everything else. Her "illness," as Mom and Dad call it, is like a bunch of dominoes lined up in a row, ready to topple over.

I don't know what set the whole row of dominoes into motion—what made Mom take that second sip after the first sip, and then the third sip after that. Whatever it was, I feel like *I'm* a domino now, with life pushing me forward and the ground rising up to meet me.

With everything falling down.

That's why, once Mom gets home, I have to work as hard as I can to keep things as normal as possible for her. And a big part of that normal is softball. It's what we do together. It's what we share. And, once I get through all this pressure and worry (which I know will totally fade away), it will still be what we both love.

Once I make the All-Star team, Mom will be so happy and proud that those dominoes will be glued to the ground. She'll never want to go back to drinking again.

Never ever.

I settle at our usual lunch table and stare at the slice of limp pizza in front of me. My friends went to the bathroom after class, so there's no one to ask me what's wrong. Just like there's no one to ask me what's wrong at home, either.

I feel like I'm in that old rental car again, stuck in the in-between place. If anyone was looking out their window at me, they might see a sunny smile on my face.

They might see a girl picking up her pizza and taking a bite, then washing it down with a sip of water.

They might see her greeting her friends when they finally arrive, and giggling with them over a shared inside joke.

They might imagine she was someone without a care in the world.

They'd be wrong.

Sixteen

I rush home right after school. We don't have softball on Tuesdays, and I use the "I have a ton of homework" excuse to explain why I can't go to Claudia's to hang out. In reality, I just want more time to plan out how to explain everything to Claudia. Even though I know she'll be fine (I think), I still want to get the words right. It's like how Mrs. Fink tells us to plan out our essays before we write them. If we don't get our ideas down first, the final product will just end up being a scribbly, murky mess.

Life is enough of a murky mess already.

I'm working—*trying* to work, actually—on my assignment for tonight when Dad comes home. Mrs. Fink told us to write about a courageous act, and I'm stumped. I don't want to pick an activist or a president or someone that everyone else will choose. I want to be original.

My brain isn't cooperating, though.

"Do you have any ideas?" I ask Dad as he rummages through the fridge. Maybe he'll sit down and help me and then we'll be so bonded that he'll tell me his big secret. Maybe.

All Dad does is pour himself a glass of pink lemonade and lean against the counter. "What about me?" He strikes a wrestler pose. "Did I ever tell you about the time I wrestled a lion? Or climbed Mount Everest?"

"Dad," I groan. When I was a kid, he used to tell me super-exaggerated bedtime stories about his adventurous life. He was a spy, a superhero, and a pioneer. He swam with sharks and rode on elephants. Of course, because he was my dad (and because I was a kid), I believed him. I laughed.

Today, though, I am *not* in the mood. "Daaaaad." I draw the word out. "I'm too old for those stories now. Mrs. Fink wants us to talk about what it means to be courageous in *real* life."

"Hmm." Dad leans back in his chair and arranges his feet on the one next to him, right on top of the blue-and-white-checked cushions that Mom bought last year.

If Mom were here right now, she'd have yelled at him: "Put your feet down! This isn't a zoo!" She's yelled those same words tons of times before—when Dad forgets to close the cabinet doors and when he tracks grass clippings into the house after cutting the lawn.

Mom always says it with a smile, of course; it's not like she's *really* mad at Dad. But I could always tell that she was *kind of* serious. That's why Dad always put his feet down right away.

Today, though, Dad's feet stay up on the chair, even as Mom's words whisper in my ear.

This isn't a zoo!

I don't say anything, though. And obviously Mom's not here to chide Dad. So his feet stay up, his toes wiggling in the air, his yellow socks too bright for my grumpy mood.

"I have an idea . . ." Dad trails off, his eyes twinkling mysteriously. "Someone you're related to, even."

"Really?" I lean forward. "Has anyone led a protest or backpacked around the world? That'd be exciting."

Dad shakes his head. "Nope. Nothing like that."

I tap my pencil against the paper. "Is the person super famous?" I look at Dad hopefully, but he shakes his head. I sigh. "Has anyone even saved a kitten in this family?"

"Oh! I did!" Dad's eyes brighten, and he reaches out and steals a cracker from the pile in front of me. "When I was a boy. There was a stray kitten in the woods behind my house and my friend John and I brought it to the veterinarian. She adopted it and everything." His eyes crinkle up. "I think that story made your mother fall in love with me."

I roll my eyes, but my heart still does a little leap at the thought of my parents being in love. Maybe they're *not* getting a divorce. "I'll do my project on you and your eight-year-old heroics. I'm sure I'll get an A."

"I was actually ten."

"Because *that* makes all the difference." I pick my backpack up off the floor, then sling it over my shoulder. "Was it the Queen of England's kitten by any chance? Did you cross a rickety bridge to get the kitten? That might help."

"Veronica." Dad motions for me to sit down again. I don't have the energy to fight.

"Courage isn't just saving kittens from bridges, you know."

I sigh, then sit back down. "I know." I quote the words Mom and Dad have told me seven bajillion times over the years. "Courage means doing something even though you're scared."

It's what they told me when I stepped behind the plate during my first softball game.

It's what they told me when we went to the amusement park and I refused to go on any of the roller coasters, even the little one that my six-year-old cousin rode over and over.

It's what Dad is telling me now in his "official lecture" voice.

"What about your mother?" Dad straightens up and puts his feet on the floor, like by invoking her name he's finally remembered the house rules.

"What about her?"

"*She's* brave."

I try to figure out how to word this so I don't get in trouble. "But Mom has an addiction, Dad. You both told me that she's struggling. How is that brave?"

I imagine researching Mom's past "issues," or listing all the times she's let me down. I don't think it would all fit on this one sheet of paper.

"It's the very definition of brave." Dad sounds like he's trying to convince himself, though, like he's reciting from a textbook.

I roll my eyes.

"Your mother *is* struggling, but she's still working to get better. She's doing something that's extremely hard for her, and she—the Mom that you and I know is still in there—is fighting back against her addiction. Every day. Every minute."

But she wasn't strong enough to do it on her own.

But she had to ask for help.

"I thought you were mad at Mom." I cross my arms over my chest.

"I'm not . . ." Dad trails off. "Okay, you're right. I *was* mad at her. I *am* mad at her."

Then why aren't you as upset as me?

I don't know how to ask that, though. Because I don't want Dad to know how upset I am. I'm afraid that if I let my feelings out, there will be no way for them to get back inside me.

They'll grow bigger and bigger until they take over the world.

"I've been angry at your mother for awhile, actually," Dad admits.

"You have?"

"For more than a year now. Ever since . . . things got really bad. You probably heard us fight, huh?" Dad gives me a wry smile.

"Yeah." I wince as I remember the last big fight, which ended with two slammed doors and Mom storming out to her car.

Dad reaches for my hand and squeezes it. "To be honest, I'm more relieved than angry now. Tired, too. I'm just glad she's getting help."

Dad's hand is warm. I don't squeeze it back, but I don't pull it away. I may still be angry at Mom and Dad, but it's nice to have *one* of my parents close.

"I've actually been going to see someone," he adds. "To talk about how I feel. Which has been helping me feel differently."

"A therapist? Like Mom's seeing?"

"Kind of." Dad nods. "It's someone that Pine Knolls recommended. Mom didn't get sick in a vacuum, after all."

I picture our heavy-duty vacuum cleaner. "What do you mean?"

Dad gives me a gentle smile. "It means that Mom didn't get sick all on her own. That she was the one who did certain actions, yes, but that we may have done things that weren't helpful to her. That we'll need to adjust our family dynamics in the future if we want to maximize her chance for healing."

"Maximize her chance for healing." It *sounds* like something a therapist would say. "So you mean that I *did* cause this?" It feels like Dad dropped a heavy brick onto my chest.

"No! I don't mean that at all." Dad pauses, his finger to

his chin, then starts again. "Do you remember the three months before Grandpa died, when he stayed here for awhile? Do you remember how stressed we all got?"

I nod. "I had to sleep on the couch."

"Exactly." Dad nods. "And I was always super cranky."

"So are you blaming Grandpa for getting sick?"

"Of course not! I'm not blaming your mom, either." Dad pulls back to look at me. "I'm just trying to explain how specific actions and moods can affect others. For example, if your mom was already stressed from work, and *then* we got in a fight, those two things together could have made her want to drink." He rubs his eyes. "Which is why when she gets out we both need to be careful to—"

"To not get mad at her?" I cross then uncross my legs. My entire body feels jittery. "I don't know if I can do that."

"We won't be perfect." Dad's voice is still gentle, which makes me grit my teeth. "And Mom's actions will never be our fault. But we do need to think about how our actions may affect her." He twiddles his thumbs. "You could talk to someone, too, if you wanted. There are groups out there specifically for kids dealing with . . . your mom's problem."

Dad can barely say the word.

It's not a "problem," Dad. It's alcoholism. Mom drinks too much. You may say that she's brave, but do you really believe it if you can't even speak the truth? If you can talk to a therapist about what happened, but not to me?

106

His anger may be fading, but mine is still as vivid as ever.

I shake my head as Dad continues talking about Mom's strength and courage and blah blah blah. Because right now I don't want a lecture on how awesome Mom is. I want to finish this assignment and go to bed. To start the day over tomorrow. To go to music class and get to sing. To go to softball practice and zone out. To be anyone but the girl with the alcoholic mother.

"Maybe writing about Mom would be too personal," I finally mutter.

Dad drums his fingers on the table, his eyes softening. I'm already bracing myself for another therapy suggestion when he surprises me. "What about your Great-Grandma Rose?"

"Great-Grandma Rose?" I search my memory, trying to remember who she is or what she looks like. "Have I seen a picture of her before?"

"Maybe?" Dad holds up a finger. "Hold on a second."

He's back in a few minutes, a scratched-up photo album in his hand, which he spreads out in front of me. I watch as he rifles through the pages, the pictures transforming from color to black-and-white as he nears the back of the album. "Here!" he exclaims, pointing to a faded photograph of a curly-haired woman in a white-and-red uniform, a baseball bat held over her right shoulder.

"She was a softball player, too?" I exclaim.

"Baseball, actually." Dad points at the logo on her uniform, a tightly fitting jersey and a matching short skirt.

I look closer. "All-American Girls Baseball League," I read aloud. "She was one of those female players during World War Two? Like in that movie Mom loves so much?"

"*A League of Their Own*," Dad says with a smile. "It's your mother's favorite."

"I remember." I smile, too, thinking about the night we curled up together on the couch, a bowl of popcorn in my lap, Mom practically bouncing out of her seat next to me.

"I can't wait for you to see this!" she exclaimed. "There's girl power and amazing baseball and even songs!"

Her eyes didn't leave the television for the entire movie, and her clear voice rose as the members of the Rockford Peaches sang their team anthem.

"The time has come for one and all . . . to play ball!"

Sometimes, before practice, we sang the line to each other, then shared a knowing laugh.

"Great-Grandma Rose was one of those players? Why didn't anyone ever tell me?"

Dad shrugs, a veil of sadness slowly descending onto his face. "Your mom only found out herself about six months ago, when Grandma Kathy was cleaning out her house and found all this memorabilia. I guess Great-Grandma Rose didn't talk about it much. We were planning on mentioning it to you, but . . . things got in the way."

Mom's drinking got in the way.

I know what Dad meant to say.

What he didn't say.

I block the thought out of my mind and point to another picture. "Wow! She played baseball while the men went to war." I read on, already planning my essay in my head.

Even though my great-grandmother wasn't risking her life by fighting, I bet she was nervous on that ball field. I bet people made fun of her for doing what everyone thought of as a "boy sport." I bet playing in front of hundreds of people and hearing about herself on the radio was scary.

I bet trying out for an entirely new league was scary.

Trying out for the All-Star team is scary enough.

I start writing notes, pushing Dad's lecture on Mom out of my mind. "Thanks, Dad," I say.

"You're welcome, honey. Glad to help." Dad ruffles my hair like I'm a little kid, then gives me a soft smile.

I grin back up at him, then freeze. Am I still mad at him? *Should* I be? What about Mom? I wish there was a rulebook for this whole thing.

Dad doesn't seem to notice my hesitation, though. "We'll figure out dinner in a bit. I have a phone call to make."

"To your therapist?" My eyes widen. "Oh! Is that where you've been? After school? And in the morning?"

"After school, yes." Dad nods. He doesn't say anything else.

"What about this morning?"

"Work stuff. Which is what I have to do now, too."

I stare at Dad more closely. I recognize that tone in his voice—it's the one he uses when he has a secret he doesn't want to share. The one he uses at Christmastime when he goes on a secret shopping outing, then bustles into the house with an obviously hidden package under his coat.

The one he used when he surprised Mom with a trip to Maine for their tenth anniversary, and Grandma Helen and Grandpa John showed up to stay with me for the weekend.

The one they *both* used when they tried to hide Mom's alcoholism this past year.

I bet Dad expects me to go along with his lies again, to sit back and ignore his bad acting. Today, though, after everything that's happened, I won't let one more secret slide by.

"Can you tell me the truth for once?" I demand, forcing my voice not to shake.

Dad's eyes widen, like I've grown three sizes into some big green monster, with sharp dripping fangs and everything.

I guess I look scary enough, because Dad shrinks before me. He looks exhausted, like he's just run a marathon. Maybe one of those ultramarathons my gym teacher does, where she runs one hundred miles at a time.

"You're right." Dad rubs his eyes. "I'm not telling you the truth."

Seventeen

Any other time, I might have done a victory dance or yelled out "Gotcha!" Today there's nothing to celebrate, though. Because I know what's coming won't be good.

Nothing *has* been good lately, so why should I expect anything different?

"I've been looking for another job," Dad says.

My eyes widen. "Did you get fired?"

Dad shakes his head. "No, nothing like that. I'm still working at my regular job and doing sales."

"Then why do you need *another* one?"

Dad looks at the ceiling. He looks at the floor. He looks anywhere but at me. "Because we need more money, sweetheart. Because even with insurance, Mom's treatment costs money. A lot of money. And after your mother comes home, I'm not sure that her work will be the best environment for her."

"Oh." Now *I* look at the floor, too. When I was a kid,

I used to try to make patterns out of the shapes on the tiles, the squares and rectangles fitting together to make all sorts of buildings and animals.

Now I just see lines. Boring blocks. Nothing's fitting together right now, either before my eyes or in my head.

"So that's why you had that meeting?" I ask.

"Yup." Dad nods. "And this phone call. I had a few interviews, and I think I've just about lined up a job at the hardware store in town."

"Big Bob's Hardware?" I ask, picturing the small storefront between KJ's Coffee and the dry cleaners.

"That's the one!" Dad forces an excited tone into his voice. "I'll be working there a few mornings stocking the shelves and on the weekends at the register. It'll be fun."

I think of Dad's life now, of all the time he spends on the phone, the trips he makes across the state, and the conferences he goes to a few times a year. "Do you have . . . time for all that?" I ask. "When will you sleep?"

Or be here?

"I'll manage." Dad stifles a yawn. "I *have* to manage. But I have to go, too. Bob will be calling any minute."

"Okay," I say slowly. "I'm sorry, Dad. I'm sorry you have to get another job, I mean. I wish I could help."

I do, too. I'm not that mad at Dad anymore. He was only keeping this secret so I wouldn't worry. Just like I don't want *him* to worry about me, either. That's why I've been hiding how much I cry at night. And how nervous I am about tryouts.

Then I have an idea. "Hey! Maybe *I* could get a job instead!"

Dad shakes his head. "Oh, Veronica, thank you for the thought, but you're too young for that." He gives me a hug. "We'll be okay. I promise."

"I want to help, though!" I exclaim. "I *can* help."

"You are helping." Dad squeezes tighter, then pulls back to look at me. "Just by being you. There is one thing, though." He takes a deep breath. "One thing that you *may* have to do to help us out. Maybe. I'm not sure yet."

Dad's words come out fast, like he's giving a speech he's so nervous about that he memorized it and practiced it five billion times.

"What is it?" I hold my breath. It feels like something's creeping alongside me, just in the corner of my vision. I *think* I know what it is, but I can't quite make it out. It's still in shadow, like in some super-creepy horror movie.

"We may not be able to afford the All-Star team, Veronica," Dad says. "Between the cost of the new uniforms and all the other fees . . . well, it's a lot of money."

Dad blabbers on, but I've stopped listening. My entire body is frozen.

Mom and I *planned* for me to do the All-Star team. Softball is what we do together. That means it would totally mess up our *dynamics* if I stopped playing.

I have to do softball for me, too. What would I do without it?

You could sing, a little voice whispers in my head, but I

quickly muffle it. Singing is just for fun. It isn't who I am. Who this *family* is.

"I have to do the All-Star team!" I plead. "I mean, I have to try out, at least."

Dad shakes his head sadly. "I know this has been your dream, Veronica, but it may not work out. Not this year."

"You said it's because the team will cost money." I feel like I'm hanging on to the side of a cliff by my fingertips, trying not to fall into the void below. "But isn't that why you're getting another job? Won't that help?"

Dad gives me a sad smile. "The job is to help pay for your mother's treatment." He says the word *treatment* like it's fragile, like if he stops worrying about Mom for one second, she'll break into pieces.

But what about me? Shouldn't *I* be handled with care, too? And softball is *my* way to help, to anchor Mom in what we—in what *she*—used to be.

"How much money could Pine Knolls even cost?" I ask.

Dad sighs. "More than you'd think."

I grit my teeth together. It's such a "parent" answer. An "I don't think you're old enough to deal with this" answer. But shouldn't Dad *know* by now that I can handle a lot? That Mom's "problem" has made me learn to do that?

"But . . . but . . . then *softball* can't be that much money. And if I can't get a *real* job, then maybe I can do something else to help with the team costs. Like babysit? Or do odd jobs?" My mind flails about for solutions, even though the thought of changing diapers makes me gri-mace. I have to think of *something*.

"It's not just the money, sweetheart." Dad rubs his eyes. "There are a lot of other factors involved in this."

"Then what are they?" I demand. Ms. Beatty always tells us that we need to know all the factors before we start working on a math problem. It's only fair that Dad follow this rule, too.

Dad's voice hardens. "Veronica Elizabeth, watch your tone."

I run my fingertip along a grain of wood on the table. "Sorry." We got this table when I turned ten, when Mom and Dad decided that I was past the age when they'd have to worry about me drawing on things with permanent marker. It's big and shiny and has these cool table legs that curl up at the bottom. (And no, I haven't ruined it yet.)

I wonder if my parents realize the irony of *Mom* being the one to ruin everything.

"It's not just the *cost* of softball," Dad continues. "It's the travel, too." I open my mouth to argue, but he holds up a hand. "Let me finish."

I nod but keep the grumptastic expression on my face.

"I can't drive you to all your practices and games if I'm juggling two jobs *and* helping to manage your mom's appointments."

I *do* remember Dad telling me how Mom will have to go to support groups and therapist appointments basically every day once she's released. "Can't Mom handle all that herself? She *is* a grown-up." I point to the big calendar on the side of the refrigerator, the one Mom says she'd fall apart without. It has all our birthdays and dentist appointments on it. Mom even schedules the times she's going to food shop each week. "She can write her meetings there."

"She can. And she might." Dad's voice is gentle. "But I want to make sure your mother has as little stress as possible when she's discharged. Her brain will still be shaky, and she may need encouragement to go to her support meetings. She may need a break from work—or even to change jobs." He puts his hand on my shoulder. "I have to be here for her, honey."

Her, but not *you*.

"What about Claudia's mom?" I ask. I feel like I've swum over my head and am splashing around for anything to hold on to. "I'm sure she can drive me."

Then I remember the separation. That Claudia's family is going through a lot right now, too. Dad's already shaking his head anyway. "I can't ask that much of another family."

I squeeze my eyes shut, coaching myself to keep the tears back and stay strong.

Dad gives me a hug. "I know this stinks, Veronica. And there is a small chance that I'm worrying for nothing. Your mother may want to keep her job. She could leave rehab and do amazingly." His bites his lip, his eyes sad. "I just have to plan for everything."

"So you don't think Mom will recover?" I don't know

if I want the answer to this question, but I still have to ask it.

"Of course I do!" Dad squeezes my hand. "I believe in your mother. But I also have to think of all the possibilities. Let's wait and see," Dad says. "You can try out for the team still. We'll know more in a few weeks."

I nod. I want to argue more, to ask him if I'm supposed to make the team, get all excited, and then . . . quit when he tells me to? How does he expect me to do that?

Dad's eyes are steely and his mouth is set, though. It's his "I'm done talking" expression. His "nothing you say can change my mind" face.

All I can do is work hard and make the team.

I can refuse to give up, too. Because there's got to be some way I can make that money. Then cross my fingers that Mom will be "recovered enough" for me to play.

"Oh!" Dad looks at the clock on the stove and jumps. "Bob will be calling any minute. I have to go. And Veronica?" He's halfway down the hallway when he looks back. "Thanks for being so mature about this."

I don't answer, but when Dad turns around again I stick my tongue out at his back.

Eighteen

No softball. No softball.

The words in my head drown out the music pulsing through my headphones. I scroll down to my favorite song, the one that came out this past fall and everyone got totally obsessed with. Claudia and I watched the music video millions of times and practiced the dance until we could do it perfectly. We sang it so much that Tabitha and Lauren banned it from their presence.

"Enough is enough." I remember Tabitha standing by the edge of the town pond on that super-hot day last October, her hands on her hips as she flicked a bug off her red-polka-dot bikini. Tabitha was the first one of us to wear an official bikini instead of the tankinis and racing suits the rest of us had been wearing for ages. Tabitha's bikini was *official* official, the kind that looked like it had been made for her body. It fit the curves she'd been developing throughout the year and the breasts that had suddenly (or so it seemed) popped up overnight.

It was barely hot enough to go swimming, but we'd all flocked to the pond anyway. Our middle school doesn't have air conditioning, so I'd felt like a limp vegetable floating through a vat of hot soup the entire day. Even if the pond was freezing, and even if the muck at the bottom felt like oozy leaves, I still needed to be in the water.

Non-bikini and all.

I kept sneaking peeks at Tabitha as I sang and danced. Tabitha looked so grown-up. Not like an adult, of course. Tabitha was way too short for that. But like a teenager, for sure. Way more of a teenager than I'd probably look for years and years.

Mom had reassured me later that she'd been the same way as a kid, too, and that it was "perfectly normal" to "develop later than your peers." Mom said it with air quotes and everything, just like our health teacher did with the official body parts when he gave us the "You're Growing Up" lecture.

Mom explained genetics to me then—how we get certain traits from each of our parents and are like them in certain ways. Like how my nose is a little turned up, like Dad's. Or how I'm good at softball, like Mom. My singing may even be genetic—Dad's cousin Nina has been in a bunch of off-Broadway shows.

"And how we both love chocolate?" I'd asked.

"Absolutely." Mom grinned, then we went into the kitchen and opened a bag of Hershey's Kisses.

The chocolate tasted good, but the reassurance that I wasn't some weird flat-chested freak felt better. I knew that my life was on the right path, even if I wasn't as . . . bust-tastic as Tabitha. I knew that Mom had been down that same path before. She'd pushed through the thorns and brambles and emerged on the other side. She'd survived being flat as a board. (Flatter than a board, even. Because boards have bumps and stuff.)

I'd survive, too. Especially if I had Claudia with me.

Baby, baby, it's gonna be all right.

I turn up the volume and sing along. I'm too upset to do the dance moves, but I still imagine them in my head. I remember twirling around my bedroom and shimmying by the pond. I remember singing the lyrics with Claudia before our softball games to pump ourselves up.

I also remember blasting it to distract myself when Mom stayed out late with her coworkers because "they invited me to a bar and it would be rude if I said no."

Stop and take a minute.

Appreciate this life.

You're in it.

Love it all.

Hug it all.

You did it.

"What do these dumb words even mean?" I grump at my empty room. "It sounds like one of those greeting cards Grandma and Papa send me for my birthday, with the watercolor flowers on the front and the mushy message inside."

I look at the icon of the album cover on my phone. "Have you even suffered a day in your life?" I ask the singer, then wrinkle my nose at her bubblegum-pink outfit and sparkly smile.

This is what I've been reduced to: taunting my phone.

Love it all.

Hug it all.

You did it.

She repeats the chorus, and I rip my headphones off, then pick up my softball glove from the end of my bed and throw it across the room.

"I didn't *do* anything! I won't *get* to do anything, either!" I picture my friends on the softball field, wearing those cool All-Star uniforms under the lights.

Singing isn't helping today. Even moping isn't helping today. The only thing that would help is a time machine that could take me back to when stupid alcohol was invented.

"Stupid money. Stupid Dad. Stupid Mom." If anyone overheard me right now, they'd think I was a preschooler throwing a tantrum. But maybe those little kids have the right idea. Because right now, anger is filling my body like one of those sand-art projects I did at camp a few years ago. Except instead of different pretty pastel colors, my sand is all red. Dark, dark red, the color of fire. Of fury.

Right now I feel angry at everyone. Every single person

and animal and creature that has ever inhabited this planet.

"Even you!" I shout at the ladybug climbing up the outside of my window. "It's *your* fault, too!" I switch to another song, this one a loud one, with lots of drums and percussion. I belt out the lyrics at the top of my lungs, daring Dad to come in and tell me to be quiet. After a few minutes, the anger swirling in my chest starts to seep down the drain. All the rest of my emotions do, too, and by the end of the song, I'm lying on my bed, every bit of me totally exhausted.

At that moment, all I want to do is talk to Claudia. Even though I've kept the truth about Mom from her so far, even though I *thought* it would be okay to hold it close inside me until the worst is over, I suddenly want to talk to my best friend so much that I ache inside.

The phone barely rings once before Claudia picks up. "Hello?"

The words catch in my throat. I don't say anything. I *can't* say anything.

"Veronica?"

A second ago, I imagined Claudia telling me that everything would be okay. But what if she *doesn't* say that? What if my big secret makes Claudia look at me differently, like I stepped into an alternate dimension and came back a total stranger?

I think about hanging up, then realize that would be pointless. Claudia *knows* it's me calling. My name is on her screen. The ringtone she assigned to me, a high tinkling of wind chimes, rang through her room or her kitchen or wherever she is.

Mom and Dad sometimes talk about when they were kids, when the technology "wasn't like it is today." They tell me how lucky I am to have my own cell phone and DVR ("You can find any show at the click of a button! No worrying about getting home in time!"). They gush about their love for caller ID, so we can avoid those annoying telemarketers who try to call during dinnertime.

And yeah, those telemarketers do stink. But right now, caller ID is preventing me from chickening out like I want to.

"Yep. It's me," I say with a resigned sigh.

"What's up?" Claudia asks. I hear the murmured voice of her mom in the background.

"Nothing really," I start. I should ease into this. Maybe talk about going to see that new Marvel movie this weekend. Or about the YouTube video of the owl wearing sunglasses I saw the other day. My mouth opens and closes, but nothing about superheroes or beach-loving birds comes out. I don't *want* to talk about meaningless stuff. I need my best friend to make me feel better.

And she will, of course. I know she will.

"So something hap—"

"What'd you say, Mom?" Claudia's voice sounds muffled, then gets louder again. "Hold on one second, Veronica. Mom's having . . . an issue."

"Oh. Sure." Random bits of their conversation make their way to my ear.

"Your father *decided that . . ."*

"Not what we discussed . . ."

"But, Mom! Veronica probably wants to . . ."

"Fine!"

I hear Claudia stomping through the house and a door slamming shut. "Ugh, my mother is driving me crazy."

"Oh no." My voice is flat, and I try to inject a little bit more sympathy into my voice. It's not Claudia's fault that her mom picked the worst time possible to get upset. "I mean, that stinks. Is everything okay?"

"Not really." I imagine Claudia on the other end on the line, slumped against the dozen decorative pillows on her bed. Claudia wants to be an oceanographer when she grows up, so her room is decorated in an ocean theme. She has tons of sea-life pillows—dolphins and otters and seahorses and fish—and there's a picture of some famous oceanographer on the wall, right next to a poster of a softball diamond.

I have the same poster in my room, too, but I don't have all the other random stuff that Claudia does. There's no balance. The softball magazines and pennants on my wall could be part of a museum exhibit labeled SOFTBALL IS MY LIFE.

I wonder if Claudia would be as devastated as me if she couldn't play on the All-Star team, or if she'd just do something else. If she *could* do something else without feeling . . . wrong.

"Dad came over this morning to pick up some more of his stuff." Claudia sniffles. "He wanted to take me and Jamie to some rock-climbing place, but Mom said it was too dangerous for Jamie." I imagine Claudia's parents playing tug-of-war, each of them holding tight to their kids' arms. "They were yelling at each other so loudly that Jamie started crying."

"Is he okay now?" I silently yell at myself. I wish I could do more than ask if her family is okay. They're obviously not okay. I don't know what else to say, though. I don't want to say the wrong thing and make Claudia feel even worse.

Like people might do to me if they find out about Mom.

"No. Well, maybe." Claudia blows her nose. "Dad told him he'd take us for doughnuts instead and Jamie perked right up." Her voice rises. "It was a total sugar bribe, but Jamie still fell for it. He's out with Dad now."

"And you're not?"

"No. Mom was still so upset at Dad that I felt bad going with them. I didn't want her to think *both* her kids were abandoning her." I hear Mrs. Munichiello's voice again. "One second, Mom!"

"You still there?"

Claudia lowers her voice. "Yeah. I mean, I'm not mad at Dad. He didn't do anything wrong . . . I think. Rock climbing *was* a cool idea. And I like doughnuts." She lets out a rough laugh. "I feel like I'm in a movie—or in someone else's life."

"I know how you feel," I say under my breath, then add "I'm so sorry" in a louder voice.

I don't know if that's the right thing to say, but at least Claudia isn't crying. Her sniffles haven't transformed into sobs.

She even lets out a half laugh, half groan. "Now she wants me to go to yoga with her, even though she knows I hate yoga."

My mind is whirling. How can I add to Claudia's worries? Telling her about Mom would be like stacking a brick onto one of those model houses we used to make out of milk cartons. *Smush!* Claudia's walls would collapse in a second.

I'd be the worst best friend ever.

"It's okay."

Okay. I think I've said that word more lately than I have in my entire life.

"Were you calling to get in some extra practice?" Claudia sighs. "I wish I could go. We need more work before tryouts."

Do we? I'm about to protest, then realize it doesn't really matter. Not today. Maybe not ever. And at least Claudia had given me an excuse about why I was calling.

"Oh, yeah. I *was* calling about heading down to the fields, but we can do something another day. Go be with your mom."

Claudia sniffles. "Are you sure?"

"Absolutely." I feel a twinge of guilt at my lie, but a teeny-tiny fib isn't *that* bad, right? I *could* be calling about softball. I just wasn't today. And not telling Claudia about Mom isn't me *lying*, it's just me shielding her from the truth.

Really, I'm Claudia's knight in shining armor.

"Go do a downward dog for me. Or is it a cat?"

Claudia snorts. "I should make up my own poses. It'd make that slow class way more fun. What about an upward leopard?"

"A flipping ferret?"

"An inverse iguana?"

"You win!" I giggle, because even though I didn't tell Claudia the truth—not yet, at least—it's still good to talk to her.

"We'll catch up later?" Claudia asks. "Maybe we can go to the field tomorrow?"

"Definitely." I nod, even though she can't see me, then hear Mrs. Munichiello yelling again.

"She's so needy," Claudia mutters. "I should go. Bye, Veronica."

"Bye," I say, but she's already hung up. Which is good, because now I don't have to resist the urge to snap back at her. To yell that I'd give anything for a needy mom. Anything for a mom to go to yoga with.

Anything for a mom who was here with me right now.

I try to do my homework until I finally hear Dad make

his usual "going to bed" noises. The *creakity creak* of him walking up the stairs. The slow whine of his "I need to oil this" bedroom door as he closes it. The too-hard *slam!* of his pajama drawer.

He's in bed early tonight, probably because he has to wake up early to work at the hardware store. Tomorrow is his first day. I can't sleep, and after a full hour of tossing and turning and groaning about how awful everything is, I carefully get out of bed and grab my glove and a softball from the floor.

I creep through the hallway and down the stairs, making sure to avoid the squeaky spot on the third stair from the bottom. I put on my sneakers and escape into the night.

I've never snuck out of the house before. Maybe before I was too young for it. I'm just getting my teenage angst now. I was the complete opposite of Tabitha's older sister, Liz. She's seventeen and sneaks out all the time.

I feel appropriately angsty tonight, though. Once I'm outside, I stomp down the street by the glow of the dim streetlights. I throw my ball in the air and squeeze it tight in my glove. When I get to the park a few blocks away, the moon shines bright above me as I make my way to the far corner, where they set up two batting cages and a backstop a few years ago. They named it the Clancy Center, after an older guy who volunteered with the town softball program for years and years.

Mom and I used to come here all the time. I'd put on a

helmet (my favorite was the shiny red one) and step into the cage, my bat held over my shoulder, my eye on the machine about to spew dozens of balls at me.

"Hold the bat higher," she'd instruct.

"Choke up more."

"Remember to step when you hit. That's how you get your power."

We'd move over to the grass and play catch next, the *thwack-putt* sound of the ball nestling into our gloves more comforting than any lullaby.

I don't have a partner tonight, so all I'm left with is the backstop, a metal frame with a mesh web stretched over it. I throw the ball over and over, catching it each time it bounces back at me.

I throw it hard.

The backstop doesn't have Mom's reflexes or accuracy, though. Sometimes my ball comes back to me at an angle; sometimes it bounces weird and goes somewhere I can't reach it at all.

I don't know what to expect or how I should be reacting.

It's not consistent.

But then again, Mom hasn't been consistent lately, either.

Maybe this is why growing up is filled with so much angst. No one's coddling me anymore, telling me that nap time is in an hour and playtime comes right after. Life doesn't work like that anymore.

Balls can hit you in the face and mothers can become alcoholics.

Parents can let you down in all sorts of ways.

I throw the ball at the backstop and it bounces to the left. I don't even try to catch it. Instead, I sit down on the ground and tilt my head toward the sky.

Above me, the moon and the stars are silent.

Nineteen

"Do you think we should get sequins on our uniforms?" Bethany Hayes runs up beside me during our pre-practice laps, her long red ponytail bouncing against her back. Bethany, the self-proclaimed "most stylish" girl in our grade, plays center field for our rec team and always finds some way to decorate her uniform. Or herself. Mr. Robertson always finds his *own* way to *un*-decorate Bethany's uniform, but he can't stop her from lacing shiny gold ribbons in her braids or putting glitter lotion all over her face.

I look down at my practice jersey, imagining it covered in pink or purple sequins—Bethany's colors of choice. "Wouldn't they jingle all over the place? Or be scratchy?" Our practice jerseys are comfy enough, but our official game uniforms are *already* super scratchy. I think the town bought them in bulk from "Cardboard Clothes R Us."

I turn the corner at the edge of the field and continue down the next straightaway. We play on the far edge of the school field, and every day before practice, Mr. Robertson makes us run two whole laps around the entire thing. I hated it at first, but now, after a full season, I totally notice how much easier running is. I think I'm faster on the bases, too, which was obviously the point.

Mr. Robertson isn't Mom, but he hasn't done an *awful* job this season. We won almost all our games *and* he taught us how to slide into home base without totally bruising our butts.

"Not *this* team's uniforms. Duh." Bethany shakes her head. *Bounce bounce swish!* goes her ponytail. "The season's almost over anyway, Veronica. That wouldn't make sense at all."

(Because softball sequins would make so much sense in general.)

"I'm talking about the All-Star uniforms," Bethany continues. "Last year they had stars on the back."

"Were the stars made out of sequins?" I try to remember last summer's All-Star uniforms. I *should* remember; I went to almost all their games. I stared at the older girls like they were rock stars, even though they were only a year or two older than me. They all seemed so grown-up, though, playing on that big field surrounded by rows and rows of bleachers and fans, fancy advertisements decorating the outfield walls. When the lights shone down on them during night games, it was like a spotlight illuminating my future.

Bethany shakes her head and giggles. "No, but they

should have been. I'm sure the coach will see how much we *need* to add some extra bling to our uniforms."

Bethany seems way too confident that she'll make the team. Then again, I feel—felt?—the same way about my chances. Now that I know we might not be able to afford All-Stars, though, Bethany's confidence seems like it's mocking me.

I dodge a pile of dog poop that someone didn't pick up, then turn my head back as the girls after me do the same. It's like some gross makeshift hurdle on our running course. Claudia vaults over the disgustingness, then catches up to us.

"Did you say *bling*?" she asks, her breath coming out in gasps. "That's the word my mom uses when she's trying to sound cool."

I snort. Well, actually snort-hack, because just then a bug flies right into my mouth. "Gack!" I skid to a halt and bend over, coughing and spitting on the grass next to me. "Ew ew ew!"

Bethany and Claudia stop, too. "What happened?" Claudia asks. "Did you pull a muscle? Sprain an ankle?"

I hack again and wave my hands in the air. "I swallowed a bug!"

"Not exactly the afternoon snack you wanted, huh?" Claudia asks with a serious face, then cracks a smile.

I start to protest that she shouldn't joke about something as disgusting as this, then realize what I must look like, spitting all over the grass and clutching at my throat.

My lips turn up and a giggle escapes my throat. The giggle turns into laughs, which transform into howls. A second later, all three of us are doubled over.

"I hope the run didn't *bug* you too much!" Bethany says through her own laughter.

"Don't you just wish you could *fly* away from here?" Claudia asks.

I give them both a high five. "I really should have *insected* this route before I ran it."

Bethany tilts her head to the side. *Flop!* goes the ponytail. "Huh?"

"*Insected?* Because it sounds like *inspected?*"

Claudia and Bethany groan. "That was bad," Claudia says.

I stick my tongue out at her as we all start running again. One more lap to go.

"Your mom is hilarious, though," Bethany says to Claudia. "And bling actually looks cool on her. Remember that sequined skirt she wore to the softball banquet last year?"

"Oh my God, that skirt." Claudia shudders. "It's better than the crop top she bought the other day, though. A crop top! She's forty-something years old and trying to shop at the same stores as me. It's so much worse since my dad moved out," Claudia continues.

I sneak a quick glance at Bethany, then back to Claudia, who nods. "It's okay, Veronica. I told Bethany."

"You . . . did?" I mean, we *know* Bethany. She's been

on our softball team all year. But it's not like she's *really* close to us. I'd expect Claudia to tell Tabitha or Lauren before Bethany.

Claudia nods. "Yeah. Her parents got divorced last year, so I knew she'd understand." She shoots me an apologetic glance. "Not that you wouldn't. Just . . . you know. Bethany gets what it's like to have a family that's not, well . . . perfect."

I turn another corner and pick up my pace. Of course Bethany would understand divorce stuff better than me. My parents are still married. And for all Claudia and Bethany know—for all Tabitha and Lauren and Mr. Robertson and my teachers and the entire *world* know—my parents are in the happiest marriage ever. Mom may be "traveling," but that's normal for some families. Everyone's parents are busy and miss games sometimes.

It should be a good thing that from the outside, everything in my life—in my family—appears fine, brushed with a rosy-pink, sparkly glow.

I should be happy that my secret is still a secret. Relieved. Dancing down the baseline.

But as Bethany and Claudia start talking behind me, about their parents fighting and sleeping in different beds and dividing up the furniture, I don't feel like dancing. The music floating across the field from the band room sounds dull and lifeless.

I want to slow down and let the girls catch up to me. I want to tell them how my mom is the furthest thing in the world from perfect. I want to tell them how much I miss her and how scared I am that she won't get better.

But then Bethany starts talking about the uniforms again, and how excited she is for this summer.

Then Claudia says that even without sequins, we'll still rock all our games, and that I'm going to be the star of the team.

And just like Mom being the "perfect mom," I want to cling to this fantasy for a bit longer.

So I run and laugh and joke, each step bringing me closer to a plan. I don't care what Dad says—I *will* play on the All-Star team this year. I'll raise the money.

Then Mom will get out of rehab in time to watch me. To cheer me on, just like she always did.

I'll make my fantasy a reality.

Twenty

"Veronica?"

There are five minutes left of lunch period and I'm rustling through my locker, trying to find my science homework, which I *thought* I'd put in here earlier but has somehow disappeared into the great black hole before me. I try to look over my shoulder but bonk my head against the locker door.

"Ow!" I pull backward and raise my hand to the rapidly forming bruise on my forehead. "This place is dangerous!"

"Sorry." Libby Kemp stands in front of me, touching her own forehead in sympathy. "I did that a few weeks ago. It's the worst."

I wince again, then pump my fist when I notice the edge of my science assignment poking out between the pages of my math book. "Sweet! I found it." I clasp the papers to my heart. "I spent hours on this dumb lab report and Ms. Davison takes ten points off for each day something's late."

"That's tough." Libby holds up her own science textbook. "Ms. Fisher's strict, but not that bad."

"Oh. Cool."

"Yeah."

"Yeah."

We stand in the hallway for a few minutes, just staring at each other. Everyone else is either in class or at lunch, so there's nothing to distract us from the awkwardness between us. I've never really talked to Libby before—I more stare in awe at her every time she plays and try to hide how jealous I am.

She looks just as nervous as me, though, which is what makes me finally speak up. "Did you . . . want something?"

Libby shuffles her feet. "Oh. Right." She giggles. "Sorry to be Admiral Awkwardsauce here. I just don't really know how to say this."

My stomach flips twice, then bounces into my throat. Is she going to tell me how I have no right thinking I could ever be on the summer team? Or is there something wrong with my outfit? Did I forget to zip my pants after going to the bathroom earlier?

I turn away, then peek down at myself. Phew!

"I saw you the other night," Libby finally says.

"The other night . . . ," I say slowly. "Which night?"

"At the park." Libby pretends to throw a ball. "At the cages and the backstop. Remember? You . . . um . . . you looked upset."

Of course I remember! I force my face into a happy expression, though. Nothing to see here, la-di-dah!

"Oh, right." I toss my hair back in my best approximation of Bethany. "That."

Think fast, Veronica, I tell myself. Give her a good reason for why you were crying in the park after dark.

Is there a good reason for crying in the park after dark?????

Maybe that's why I tell Libby the truth.

Maybe it's because Libby looks like she really cares. Maybe it's because she's not stuck in the quicksand of her own issues or squealing about sequins.

Maybe it's because Libby doesn't know me that well, so I don't have to be happy-all-the-time Veronica. All she knows is what's in front of her. Who I am *now*.

Whatever the reason, this time I don't lie. I don't make things sound better than they are.

Instead, I tell Libby everything: about my mom and her drinking, about Dad's new job and maybe not getting to play softball this spring and summer. About feeling so alone it's like I'm in the middle of a crowded room but no one can see or hear me.

"I . . . I . . ." My breath catches in my throat, the sobs rising up like a tidal wave, threatening to pull me under. "I don't know what I'll do if I can't play."

Libby's face matches my own, which reassures me that she understands the severity of the situation. Of course she understands. Libby loves softball maybe even more than I do. She's better than me, at least. I really thought I had the potential to get as good as her, though.

I just needed the practice time. Now I'm going to fall way behind.

"So that's why you were crying," Libby says. "I'd be upset, too."

"It's not just softball," I tell her, then look down as I wipe a tear from the corner of my eye. "It's more about my mom. No, actually it's both." I slam my locker door closed. The *clang* echoes through the empty hallway. The teacher in the room next to us peeks his head through the little window in his door, then retreats backward.

"You'll totally make the team," Libby assures me. "Coach Ortiz is tough, but you're good."

"It doesn't matter if I'm good if we can't afford for me to play." I lean back against the wall and close my eyes. "I just don't know what I can do to fix that. It's not like I can go work at Panera or something. Or become some super-famous Instagram influencer in a week or two."

"Strike a pose!" Libby pretends to take a picture of me, but I can't even fake a smile.

"See? There's no hashtag for what I'm going through."

Libby puts her hand on my shoulder. "There kind of is."

"Huh?"

"I mean, I get what you're going through," Libby says softly.

No, you don't *get it*, I think to myself. No one could possibly imagine what this is like unless they've been here, too.

The look on Libby's face, though, a mix of concern and sadness, makes me feel good. It makes me think that in this case, her imagination may be enough to help, if only the teensiest bit.

"Thanks." I say it softly, even though there's still no one else in the hallway to hear me. Because sometimes you have to say things softly. Things that need special care. Things that mean the most.

"I *do* get it," Libby continues. "I mean, I really get it. My mom is . . . well, she does that, too."

That's when I see the truth in Libby's eyes. The understanding. The pain.

And I get it, too.

"Is she better?" I'm not sure if I want the answer or not.

"I think so," Libby brushes a strand of hair behind her ears. A second later, it falls forward again. "I mean, she has been. For a year. Thirteen months, actually. That's how they measure it. In months."

"They?"

"At the meetings she goes to. They count how long they've been sober. How long since they've last had a drink. They talk about stuff, too. Like how hard it is not to drink." Libby makes a face.

"Is not drinking still hard for her?" Libby seems upset,

141

but I can't stop myself from asking the question. It's like she's my very own crystal ball in human form.

"Apparently. Although I don't know why it should be." Libby crosses her arms over her chest. "I worry about her a lot, though. Like when . . ." Libby shakes her head. "Never mind. Nothing happened."

"Okay . . ." I decide not to pry. Libby will tell me what's going on when she's ready. Or not. She doesn't owe me anything, after all. It was my choice to blurt out my entire life story.

"Recovery is a journey," Libby says. It sounds like she's quoting from a book, like she's fluent in a language I've just started taking classes in.

"That sounds like something my dad would say."

Libby snorts. "Ha! Mine, too."

"My dad tells how to *feel*," I say. "Like that I should *trust* Mom. Even though he doesn't seem to trust her himself," I add darkly. "And acts like everything is totally fine."

"It stinks," Libby says.

"All of it."

"One hundred percent. One *zillion* percent!"

I smile weakly. "Thanks. For listening, I mean."

Libby smiles. "No problem. I wanted to pass it on."

"Pass it on?"

"To tell you that things can get better and you're not alone. Like people did for me."

"What do you mean?"

"I go to a support group. For people who want to talk about our messed-up families." Libby shrugs. "It sounds weird, but it helps."

"So you just go and talk about your feelings and cry?" I shake my head. "Not my thing."

"That's what I said at first!" Libby exclaims. "I protested for months before Dad made me go. He said we couldn't go on vacation unless I tried it, which was totally unfair, but I guess I'm glad he blackmailed me. Because it helps."

I raise my eyebrows. "All I'm picturing is a scene from a TV show where a bunch of people gather in some big church basement and sit on metal chairs and hug each other." I hold my arms out like I'm pushing those potential huggers away. "*Not* my thing."

"It's not like that. Really." Libby smiles. "Maybe you could come to a meeting? Just one?" She shuffles back and forth on her shiny ballet flats. It's weird to see Libby so unsure of herself. Usually I'm around her on the softball field, where she's basically like a queen surveying her kingdom.

Except right now, there's no throne in sight. We're on the exact same level.

"Maybe," I echo, even though there's no way I'm going to be all mushy-gushy with a bunch of strangers.

"Cool." Libby smiles. "It usually meets on Tuesday nights. I'll text you the details."

"I can't wait." I try to make my voice sound all perky,

but even though I've been tricking everyone else lately, Libby doesn't seem fooled.

"Maybe we could get together before then," she says after a second. Her voice is unsure, her eyes flicking between my face and the ground. "We could try to figure out ways to make you that money."

"Really? You'd do that?"

A grin flashes across Libby's face. "Of course! We're friends . . . right?"

"Yeah!" I smile back. "That'd be cool." My heart beats a bit faster in my chest. "Do you really think we could make enough for me to play? *If* I make the team, I mean."

"Of *course* you'll make the team." Libby says it like she'd say the sky was blue. Or that pizza is the best food in the universe. "You're too good at softball not to play. And you love it so much."

Love it so much.

The words linger in the air. *Do* I love softball like Libby does, in the way that makes it my reason for getting up in the morning?

Then I shake my head. Of course I love softball. I'm just nervous—about tough Coach Ortiz and how the All-Star kids supposedly have to run three miles before every practice.

"We'll totally figure out how to make the money." I say the words to reassure myself as much as Libby.

"Of course we will." Libby winks. "We're good figure-things-outers."

"That's not even a word!" I laugh.

"It should be. See you after school?" Libby asks.

"After practice, you mean?" I elbow her in the side. "We're playing you guys on Saturday and you need all the practice you can get."

"Ooh, fighting words!" Libby exclaims. "And you're wrong, because we're totally going to kick your butt!"

Our debate probably could have gone on forever, but the bell rings and kids start streaming out of the cafeteria.

"Six o'clock?" Libby asks.

"At the park?"

"Perfect." Libby nods, and a tiny sprout of hope blooms in my stomach. It's not flowering yet, but it's on its way. It's not a weed, either.

"Should we invite Claudia?" Libby asks. "Since she's your best friend, I mean."

I think about how Claudia was too busy for me the other day. How it feels like she doesn't want anything to change between us, even though that's basically impossible.

"Nah." I shake my head. "I bet she's—I mean, I think she's busy."

Libby gives me a curious look, but she still heads off to class. I do, too, trying hard to ignore the guilt blooming right next to that seed of hope.

Twenty-One

"She's here again."

"What?" I twist my head toward the stands at Claudia's whisper. "Who's here?"

I know who she means, though. Who else could Claudia mean but Coach Ortiz? When I look at the stands, she's in the top row of the bleachers, her eyes hidden behind her buggy glasses. If Coach Ortiz really were a bug, she'd be a ladybug—her sunglasses are black and today she's wearing a red t-shirt with white running shorts.

I wonder if her being here is good luck. Probably not, because this ladybug looks like she's poisonous. Coach Ortiz isn't smiling at all and her posture is so straight she looks more like a ballerina than a softball player.

Making the team isn't about luck, anyway. That's one of the things Mom always told me. "I worked hard at softball, Veronica." We were sitting on the first-base line one day, taking a break from an afternoon of batting practice. "I wasn't one of those kids who was born a natural athlete. Not like my older brother, Sam. He basically came out of the womb with a basketball attached to his hand."

That's when I made a fake gagging sound. No one wants to hear their mother talking about wombs.

"Me, on the other hand . . ." Mom shook her head and traced a pattern in the dirt. "I spent *hundreds* of hours in the batting cages. *Thousands* of hours playing catch with my mom and running around our neighborhood."

Just like *we* do, I thought at the time. I remember looking up at the wispy clouds that drifted overhead. We'd been studying cloud types in school, so I knew that the ones above me were cirrus clouds, the small ones that looked like strands of cotton candy. They meant good weather ahead; sunny days with no chance of storms.

Apparently clouds don't know everything.

Mom was right, though. Hard work does pay off. Because I've never been the best natural softball player, either. I'm not Libby, who probably came out of *her* mother's womb (ew) wearing a softball glove. I run a bit slower than most of my team. I struggled at shortstop before finding out I liked third way better. And every time I get up to bat, I still have to remind myself to follow through.

I've gotten so much better, too. And I really think I can make the All-Star team. Well, in the alternate "I'll definitely be *able* to play and it will fix everything" universe.

I really don't want to give up on that universe yet.

That's why, when I see Coach Ortiz in the stands, I squeeze my eyes shut and imagine I come from a family with no problems at all. A family where it's totally expected that my parents will be at every single one of my games. Where I'm going to play awesome enough that Coach Ortiz will be dazzled by my mad skills.

"Don't scouts usually come to games instead of practices?" I whisper to Claudia.

Claudia peeks at Coach Ortiz again. "Maybe she wants to see how much we mess up in practice? Or our work ethic or whatever?"

"But practice is when we're *supposed* to mess up!" Amelia Underwood pops up by my side. "What if my throw goes wild and hits her in the face?" Her eyes open wide with horror.

"You could do that in a game, too," Claudia points out. "Why is practice any different?"

Claudia sounds calm, but I know exactly how Amelia's feeling. The "what ifs" fly through my head like wasps, threating to sting me and replace all my joy with pain. Claudia's words do nothing to make me feel any better.

At least they help Amelia. "I guess you're right. Coach Ortiz will see how we play at tryouts anyway." She runs off, leaving me staring after her. Amelia is another one of those born athletes, the girl who runs the mile faster than everyone else in gym class without even training. Maybe *she* can relax, but I sure can't.

And what if I mess up at tryouts, too?

Buzz buzz buzz.

I force myself to take a deep breath. Maybe if we start

playing, I can get my mind off my worries. "Let's go practice. We have our last game this weekend and I want to win it." I run onto the field, but with each step, I can feel Coach Ortiz's shadow looming over me.

It reminds me of the time we all went out for Mom's birthday and she drank a few too many margaritas, when I kept squirming in my seat, wondering if the tables around us were talking about how loud she was getting.

It reminds me of when I'm walking down the hallway at school, hear someone say the word *mom*, and wonder if they're talking about *my* mom.

Somehow I've transformed into a specimen under a microscope. If the rest of the world isn't analyzing me, then I'm analyzing myself and wondering what's going to happen.

I just want to live.

I just want to play and have fun, to have life be the way it always was.

But the ladybug's eyes are on my back, boring into me. Judging me as much as everyone else is.

So even as I hit and throw and catch, I wonder what I'm doing wrong.

I worry that I'm going to drop a ball. (Which I do.)

I worry that I don't hit far enough. (One time, I only hit a grounder to first.)

I worry that I'm not as fast as Claudia and Amelia. (Today, I don't feel fast at all.)

I'm better than I used to be, for sure. But am I good enough to impress Coach Ortiz?

Twenty-Two

"Dad?" I walk through the front door cautiously. "Is that you?" It's a silly question to ask, because of course I know it's Dad. I know my own father's voice. I just didn't expect to arrive home to him yelling like this. My heartbeat speeds up. Is Mom home? Are they having another fight? I hear a pause, then Dad's raised voice again.

Oh. Right. He must be on the phone. A pit opens in my stomach. Of course Mom isn't home.

Of course.

"Dad?" I call again.

"In here, honey! I'll just be a second."

"Okay." I throw my backpack by the foot of the stairs, then turn and unzip it, pulling out the apple I didn't have at lunch. I might get attacked if I go into the kitchen for a snack now.

"We're fine. I promise." Dad's voice is still loud, and he heaves a heavy sigh, the kind of Big, Bad Wolf sigh that could blow down a house of straw. "Mom, you don't have to come here. I can handle my own daughter."

I creep closer to the kitchen door, one of those swingy ones that look like the entrance to an Old West saloon. I press myself against the wall, then peek around the door. Dad is facing the window over the sink, his cell phone so close to his ear that I think it might fuse with his head. Grandma Helen and Dad don't talk on the phone that much. They're close, but Dad always says he's not a "phone person."

I've never heard him this upset with her, either.

"I can cook, too!" Dad's throws his hands in the air, then quickly brings the phone back to his ear. "I am a functioning adult, you know."

I can't hear Grandma on the other end, but I bet she's saying something about bringing over a bunch of casseroles. Stuff that neighbors and family do when you lose a loved one. Mom's not dead, though. She's going to get better and come home soon.

Unless Dad and Grandma Helen know something I don't?

Dad keeps talking, stuff about how Mom is working hard to get better. About how I'm doing fine with him working two jobs and how we "one hundred percent don't need anything."

Which is a total lie. As I look around the hasn't-been-vacuumed-in-weeks living room, I want to shout the truth at the top of my lungs.

We do need you! In so many ways.

Dad doesn't know how frustrating it is when he's at the hardware store and I need help with my homework. He doesn't know how lonely it is to heat up a microwave pizza for dinner and eat it at the table by myself while he's at the hardware store.

He doesn't know what it's like to want to tell Mom how I'm getting more and more nervous about softball by the day. How scary it is to think that Coach Ortiz is going to be judging me against the other girls. That I might *stay* that nervous and scared the entire *season* since I have to *keep* proving I'm as good as everyone else.

I probably couldn't tell Grandma Helen all that, but I could at least get a hug from her. She could at least eat dinner with me.

Why didn't Dad tell her the truth?

Is he ashamed of Mom after all?

Twenty-Three

"Maybe a bake sale?" Even as the words leave her mouth, though, Libby shakes her head. "No. Ingredients cost money, and I bet we'd need a lot of ingredients."

"Especially since I'd probably mess up a lot." I roll my eyes. "I am *not* what you'd call a master chef. One time Claudia and I tried to make brownies and I forgot to set the timer. By the time we remembered to check the oven, they were basically chocolate bricks. If I'd bitten one, I'd have lost a tooth!" My stomach is in pangs at the thought of Claudia, but I push the guilt away. She's probably busy doing homework now anyway. Or at yoga with her mom. She doesn't need—or want—to know all this.

"Bake sales are boring anyway," Libby adds. "The PTO does that kind of stuff. We need something with pizzazz. With oomph!" She wiggles her fingers in a jazz hands pose.

"With sparkle!" I lean back against the batting cage

fence to think. There's no one else around tonight, so we've set up camp behind home base, right in the dirt. "Ooh, what about the town talent show? I saw a sign for that the other day. *That's* sparkle-tastic."

"No way," Libby says quickly. "Not for me."

I picture myself up on stage in a shimmery costume and a top hat, singing and dancing. It sounds fun, but I'm probably not good enough to perform in front of a crowd. Not yet, at least. "I guess not for me, either."

Libby nods. "My one talent is softball, and I don't think hitting a line drive into the audience would be the best idea."

"An odd-jobs service?" I shudder, imagining some parent hiring us to change litter boxes. Or clean toilets. I don't know which one would be grosser.

I think Libby's thinking the same thing—her mouth is twisted up like she just ate a lemon.

"No way," she says, then hesitates. "But I was wondering . . . do you want to keep this a secret? Or do you care that other people know that we need money?" I notice that she says "we," which makes me happy. Libby lives in a big house and always has tons of new clothes, but she's not judging me for needing money.

"I guess it doesn't matter," I finally say. "I mean, every-one wants to make money, right? I bet people will just assume we want to buy candy or books or movie tickets." I think for a second. "As long as . . ."

"As long as what?" Libby rustles in her messenger bag

and pulls out two bags of Skittles, then hands one to me. "Speaking of candy."

"Ooh, thanks." I rip open the package, then pick out two reds, my favorites.

"You definitely won't tell anyone I need the money because of rehab, right? You won't do that?" I know I've asked Libby this before. I know she's reassured me she'll keep my secret. I still need to ask, though. I still need to be on guard.

I've gotten too used to people betraying me.

"Of course not!" Libby shakes her head so hard some of her brown hair falls out of her loose braid. "I promise."

"But *you* tell people."

"Only at my support group." Libby draws a circle next to her, then a cloud. "Because I know they'll understand. That's why it's nice to talk to you, too."

"Yeah." I feel the same way.

"I know it's scary to tell someone for the first time, though." Libby holds out her hand and wiggles her pinkie finger in the air. "That's why we should do a pinkie promise."

I giggle, then hook my pinkie onto hers and tug. "Pinkie promise we won't tell."

"Pinkie promise we won't tell," Libby echoes.

The last two lines of my favorite song flit into my head, and before I can stop myself, I sing them softly.

I promise, I promise.
Forever and ever.

155

"Wow!"

"Huh?" I press my lips together quickly, bottling the music back up inside me.

"You're good!"

"No way." I shake my head. "I'm okay." I get a thrill at Libby's words, though. Maybe I *am* good.

"You should totally do Chorus Club," Libby says. "I bet you'd get all the solos."

"I do!" I exclaim. "Well, Chorus Club, I mean. And I did get *some* solos. I just can't sing for the rest of the year because of All-Star practice."

"That's a bummer," Libby says. "It always looks like so much fun. I've never been able to do it because of the extra batting clinic Dad signed me up for. But I love to sing, too!" She sings a few lyrics from the song, then jumps up and does some moves from the music video.

Never gonna hold me back,
It's time to get on track.

It's not quite as good as Claudia's and my routine, but she's good!

Good enough to be on stage, for sure.

"We *should* do the talent show!" I exclaim. "You and me."

"No way," Libby says again. "We're not good enough for that!"

"We are, though!" I think about what Dad and Mom

and everyone keep telling me about softball—that even though I'm nervous about All-Stars, I'm one hundred percent talented enough to make the team. I can already tell that Libby and I are good enough to be in the show. Especially since I know there's a three-hundred-dollar grand prize!

If getting up on stage is what it will take to do softball again, then I'll dance and sing in front of the whole world.

"We can totally win, Libby."

Libby looks pale. "But . . ."

I stand up and still her trembling hands. "Like you said, we're good. And you danced in front of me just fine."

"But that was just you," Libby says weakly.

"You won't even notice the audience," I beg. "And we'll learn the moves so well that we won't mess up at all. I promise."

"Everyone will laugh at us."

"The jerks might. But everyone else will cheer."

My stomach feels a little jittery, but I can also see big dollar signs floating before my eyes. Floating uniforms, too. And cleats. Everything that I can't afford but will soon be able to. I blink and they're gone, but the idea is still there, waiting to be realized.

"Please?" I beg. "I know you'll be awesome. And I can't do this alone. I need a teammate. A friend."

Libby bites her lip. She opens and closes her mouth.

"Okay," she finally says, and I rush forward to wrap her in a hug. "I'll do it. But I'm going to be *super* nervous."

"Me too!" I promise her. "But this is a plan. A good plan. A great plan."

I can't hide the smile on my face.

I get to be a singer *and* a softball player.

I'll win the money, make the team, and then welcome Mom home for good.

Finally, I have a plan.

Twenty-Four

"Stop! Don't do it! Don't go!" My shrieks echo in my ears as I wake up with a gasp, my pajamas soaked through with sweat and my sheets tangled around my feet. I pull the top sheet around me and clutch it to my chest like a security blanket, my eyes darting around my room.

All I can see are shadows, but the emptiness in my chest makes me check that everything's still here. My desk and lamp are where they're supposed to be, as is the backpack slung over the arm of my rocking chair and the overflowing pile of stuffed animals in the corner.

Dad keeps telling me that I should start thinking about which stuffed animals and toys I want to donate, but I can never bring myself to choose between Mr. Buttons the Bunny and Grizzly the Bear. So they're both still here now, their beady little eyes staring at me out of the dark.

Everything is here.

Except the one thing that matters most.

I close my eyes, but the image from my dream looms behind my eyelids, settling in as it makes a permanent imprint upon my brain. I squeeze my eyes tighter and whimper.

"Veronica? Honey? Are you okay?" The door to my room bangs opens, and Dad barrels in, his hair night-messy and his t-shirt stained with something that looks a lot like salsa.

I pull the sheets closer to my chin and shrink back against my headboard as Dad flicks on the light. It's not that I'm scared of Dad. Or even *really* scared of the images still flashing through my brain. I know it was a bad dream. Logically, at least.

But dreams are based in reality—I learned that when I was a kid, after I had a bad softball game the same day I baked a cake with Mom. I dreamed that I was trapped in a big mixing bowl, trying to scrape off the batter on the sides with my softball bat.

This dream is no different.

"I, uh, just had a bad dream." I keep my eyes open as wide as possible. To let the light in. To let reality in, even if reality isn't much better than the darkness inside my head.

"Are you okay?" Dad's slippered feet shuffle along my rug. Dad's a big slipper guy—he wears them basically from September until June, and alternates between nor- mal boring "Dad" slippers and fuzzy animal ones that I beg him to hide whenever I have a sleepover. Today he's wearing polar bears on his feet.

"Yeah, I'm fine." I try to smile at Dad to show him I'm telling the truth, but my lips are shaky. Which is weird. Lately, I've been a master of fake smiles.

"You sure?" He sits down and looks closer.

"Total—" That's when my voice breaks, the sobs finally working their way up my throat and into the dark bedroom. They feel almost real in the air around me, ghosts whispering about what—who—is missing and gone.

I collapse into Dad's lap, my tears soaking his pant legs, the salt wetting my lips. "I miss Mom!" This isn't one of those polite crying sessions where tears drip daintily down my cheeks and my eyes get a little pinkish. This is a guttural sob, where I bend in half, my breath coming fast and my wails filling the room like an injured animal's.

"Oh, Veronica." Dad strokes my hair like he did when I was little and got scared about the monsters in my closet, the ones I was sure turned invisible whenever I opened the door. "It's okay, honey."

"It's not okay!" I'm still crying, and it doesn't feel like the tears will ever stop. I wonder if anyone has ever cried forever and ever? Maybe I'll be the first one, some medical marvel that doctors will study. I'll make it into the record books. I'll cry so much that I'll have to wear rain boots all the time so don't slip and slide all over the place.

"Mom's gone!" I sob. "She left us and she's sick and she's never going to get better."

"No, no." Dad repeats the word over and over, low and singsong like it's a lullaby lulling me to sleep. "That's not true. Yes, your mother isn't here, but it's not because she left us. It's because she's finding the part of herself that will allow her to come back to us."

I tilt my head back to look at Dad, then snuffle in a bunch of snot. "That sounds like something you read in one of your self-help books."

"I don't—" he starts to protest, but I interrupt him.

"I've seen the pile on your desk. The ones about helping Mom and helping me and helping yourself. The articles about 'supporting an alcoholic' and 'kids of alcoholics' that you keep forgetting to close on your computer. I know you're studying up."

Dad sighs. "Busted."

I snuffle-snot again. "I'm actually glad you left them out." I look down at my bedspread, too nervous to meet Dad's eyes. "I've been wanting to know more stuff. And I didn't know who to ask."

Now I wish the light was still off. This feels like the type of honesty that should only be done under a cloak of darkness.

"You could have asked me." Dad sounds hurt. Who is he kidding, though? He can't even talk to his own mother about this stuff.

"I guess." I wonder if I should tell him about Libby, or the support group she mentioned, but decide to hold back. I don't want to give up *her* secret, after all.

"You could have gone to the library, too."

I shake my head. "No way. They'd think something was wrong."

Dad clears his throat. I lift my head to meet his eyes as he gives me a knowing look. "Veronica. Something *is* wrong."

Anger rises in me when I hear those words come out of his mouth. *Now* he admits that something is wrong? *Now,* when no one else is here to hear our cry for help?

I snort.

Dad doesn't speak snort language, though, and totally misinterprets why I'm upset. "Honey, the librarians wouldn't judge you. They're not even allowed to ask questions about what you're researching." He pokes me in the side. "There are laws. The police would send them to librarian jail."

I squirm away from Dad. "It's not funny." I flop on my stomach and bury my face in my pillow.

"Okay, okay." I hear him getting up from my bed.

"Don't go!" I sit up before I even realize I'm doing it, my arms shooting out for him.

"Yes?" Dad pads back.

I bite my lip. I feel like a little kid crying out for her daddy. In a way, though, that's what I am. I don't want to be mad at Dad right now. I want him to make me feel better. About both the dream and all the stuff I read from his research, all the information that's flooding back into my head.

"All that information in your books . . ." I inch closer to dad again. "It scared me. I read about people who never got better and relapsed again and again and then they got divorced and . . ." I break off, my breath coming in gasps.

"Hey." Dad rubs my back in circles one way, then the other. "That's not going to happen to your mother." He tilts my chin up. "Is that what your dream was about?"

I nod. "Kind of." The images arise in my mind again. "Mom came home and said she was better, but then the very first night, she told us she didn't care about us anymore and was leaving." Tears prickle my eyelids again. "I woke up right after she walked out the door."

"That sounds scary." Dad's voice is serious, like he totally gets it. After all, Mom isn't just my mother, she's also his wife. Maybe Dad has nightmares, too.

"It was." My voice trembles, and even though I'm tempted to make myself sound brave, the secret is basically out. I'm tired of hiding my feelings anyway.

I'm just plain tired.

"Do you want to know a secret?" Dad waits for me to meet his eyes. "I'm scared, too."

"You are?"

"Absolutely." Dad nods. "Every day. Every minute. I've been scared since your mom started having problems with her drinking, and I've been terrified since we left her at Pine Knolls."

"But every time I act like a brat, you tell *me* not to worry!" I exclaim. "And you keep saying that everything is going to be okay."

Dad shrugs. "I'm a good actor, I guess. I'm trying to be a good dad, too—to stop *you* from worrying." He squeezes my hand. "But I guess it didn't work. I just made *myself* worry more. And I forgot to reassure you that feeling like this is totally normal."

I wipe my nose. "But what if Mom does relapse? What if she does leave us to drink?"

Dad meets my eyes, his face stern. "Veronica, I know your mother. I know that she has disappointed us both, and I know that sometimes I get so angry I could scream. But I also know that deep down, Mom didn't *want* to do any of the things she did. And now that she's in rehab, I'm one hundred percent positive that she's working as hard as she can to leave this disease behind. She may have to fight for the rest of her life, but believe me—she will fight." His eyes bear into mine. "She will."

Dad's voice is so sure that I can't help but nod. "Okay."

Dad gives me a hug. "It's okay to be *not* okay sometimes, too, though. I sure have my bad days. But we can get through this together, as long as we're honest with each other."

I start to say something about Dad keeping secrets from Grandma Helen, but he starts talking before I get the chance.

"I was just thinking of something else," he continues.

"What?"

"I know that we can't *visit* your mother for a bit longer, but now that she's been there for more than two weeks, we can write to her."

"She doesn't have computer access, though—"

Dad grins. "There are other ways of communicating besides on the computer or your phone, you know." He sighs dramatically. "You kids and your technology!"

I giggle. "So you want me to send Mom a carrier pigeon? Or a telegraph, like when you were younger, back in the horse and buggy days?"

"Watch it!" Dad pokes me back. "Or I'll make you write with a quill."

"Sure thing, old man." Then my face goes serious again. "So we can really write letters to Mom?"

"Absolutely."

Swirls of fear and excitement (fearcitement?) compete for space in my stomach as I think about sending a message to Mom. Should I tell her how Dad's worried about money? About how I keep messing up on the softball field? About my big talent show plan?

What if something I say makes her worse?

Twenty-Five

Dear Mom,

Dad says I ~~can write have to write~~ *can write to you now . . .*

~~~~~~~~~~~~~~~~~~~~~~~

Dear Mom,

Why are you still there? You said these programs usually take eight weeks, but that you were going to work really, really hard. That means that you should have been your overachiever self and finished early — one week should have done the trick. But you're not done. You're not home. That means you're not working hard after all . . .

~~~~~~~~~~~~~~~~~~~~~~~

Dear Mom,

Home isn't the same without you . . .

"Argh!" I crumple up the latest version of my letter and throw it across the room. I try to aim for my garbage can, but it doesn't even get near the rim. It lays there on the floor with all the other crushed-up balls. There's a whole family over there now.

I've been trying to write this letter for days and I've barely made it past the first paragraph. Everything sounds either too whiny or too angry. I want Mom to know I miss her, but not *too* much. I want her to know how much she hurt me, but I don't want to discourage her. I want . . .

I want her to be the old Mom, the one who used to order ginormous lobsters with me whenever we went to Cape Cod, then spent the entire meal waving those little claws at Dad while we pretended to be Lobster Lady and her sidekick, Red.

The one who knew more about Harry Potter than practically all my friends and won our town library's trivia contest wearing her Hufflepuff shirt and time-turner necklace.

The one who *should* have found a way to be in touch with me this past week, even though it was against the rules.

Because that's what moms do. They stick around. They find a way to come home, even when the rest of the world—or their own minds—are pulling them away. They don't need letters written to them, because they're already there with a hug or a kiss or even a hand squeeze.

At the very least, they magically send vibes across

town so their daughters know what to write in potentially the most important letter of their lives!

For a second, I'm tempted to yell down to Dad and ask him what I should write. I'm sure he knows the answer from one of those books he's been reading.

"Start out with how much you miss her," he'd say. "Then talk about your life. Maybe share a happy memory. Then end with how proud you are of her. How excited you are for the future."

His idea *sounded* good, like it could be read as a voice-over in some serious movie, accompanied by dramatic music. There'd be a split screen, with the mom on one side, reading the letter as tears pour down her (newly sober) face. On the other side, the daughter would be writing on fancy stationery, her tongue between her lips in concentration. She'd look up at the camera and stare into space, then smile fondly as memories washed over her. The music would swell and the picture would shift to their tearful reunion and "happily ever after."

The problem is, I can't get my pen to write those perfect words. I'm just using a plain old BIC pen, with a sheet of paper ripped out of my notebook, complete with those little fuzzies on the left side, the ones Mrs. Fink always yells at us about if we don't cut them off before turning in our homework.

"It's a sign of unprofessionalism," she says. "Messy papers show me that you don't respect your work or your audience."

I stare at the little fuzzies, then run my finger over them until they're soft and even fuzzier. I *should* have fancy stationery for this letter. I should have an expensive pen, too. Maybe one of those fountain pens with the pointy tips. It should be green ink, too, since that's Mom's favorite color.

I jump off my bed and rummage through my desk. All of a sudden, it feels like the most important thing in the world that this letter be perfect. Perfect message, perfect penmanship, perfect office supplies. Maybe I should type it. My handwriting isn't the greatest.

"Where is that paper?" I look through the top drawer of my desk, then all the side drawers. Nothing. I *know* I had stationery here somewhere. It was light blue with my name on the top in fancy cursive writing. There was a lighthouse on the bottom of every sheet, too.

My letter would look awesome on that stationery.

It has to be in there.

I check the storage boxes in the back of my closet, but all I see are old Legos, dolls, and craft supplies.

"Dad?" I poke my head out the door. My voice and my hands are both shaking.

"Yeah?"

"Do you know where my stationery is? The stuff you and Mom got me for Christmas a few years ago?" My eyes dart around the hallway, like the stationery will magically fall out of the air.

Dad's voice echoes back from down the hall. "We got you stationery?"

Of course Dad doesn't know where it is. Dad usually doesn't even buy the Christmas presents. That's Mom's job. Along with knowing where basically everything in this house is.

Mom's not here, though. Which means that no one is doing her job.

I comb through the rest of the house, my movements becoming more and more frantic. I dig through Dad's desk. I rifle through the junk drawer, tossing papers and pens on the floor.

I can't find anything, though.

I scream in frustration and pound my fists on the counters. It hurts, but it doesn't hurt as much as my heart does.

"Veronica? Are you okay?"

I don't answer. I can't answer.

I just run up the stairs and collapse onto my bed, tears leaking from the corners of my eyes. I know that I'm not crying over a few sheets of paper. Not really.

But I also *need* that lighthouse stationery. It's the only thing that will help right now, the light drawing me away from the rocks of my own sadness.

I cry until I don't have any tears left, then write letter after letter, way past my bedtime.

Twenty-Six

"And a one, two, three, four!" Libby presses PLAY on her phone and the music fills my bedroom. I strike a "hands framing my face" pose, just like the singer does in the video, then step forward into a series of complicated steps.

Forward, back, twirl. Step, back, twirl. Hop, make a face, cartwheel.

"Whoops!" Somehow I end up on my back, staring at the swirly white paint on my ceiling.

Libby collapses into giggles on my bed. "Good thing we're not trying out for the gymnastics team!"

I snort. "Seriously. I could do a cartwheel when I was little kid, but I guess it's not exactly like riding a bike."

Libby tries her own cartwheel. It looks better than mine felt, but she still ends up with her knees bent, halfway crouched on the floor. "Yeah, we're definitely not going to the Olympics."

"In gymnastics at least." I think about standing on the

podium accepting a gold medal for softball. Me and the rest of my team, of course. I couldn't win a game alone. "Do you, um, ever think about . . ."

"Going to the Olympics for softball?" Libby nods her head furiously. "All the time." She looks at me shyly. "Can you keep a secret?"

"You're keeping one for me," I point out.

"True!" Libby hesitates. "So, uh, when I was a kid, I used to set up a podium in my room and pretend it was a medal ceremony. Then I'd parade around the house with the national anthem blaring."

I laugh, which causes Libby to blush and turn away from me. "I'm not making fun of you!" I reassure her quickly. "I'm laughing because I used to do the same thing."

Libby gives me a high five. "Then I'll tell you another secret. That wasn't when I was a kid . . . it was last year."

I give her a low five, too. High five, low five, in the middle five. It's what Claudia and I always do before our games to psych ourselves up. It feels a bit disloyal doing it with Libby, but then again, it's not like Claudia and I put a patent on it. I'm allowed to make new friends, after all.

Then why do I feel so awful right now? Why haven't I told Claudia about Mom yet? I push the feeling away and bounce off the floor. "Let's try again. Maybe we don't have to do the cartwheel. I know there's one in the video, but we could substitute something else instead."

"No way." Libby shakes her head. "If we want to win this talent show, we need to do it perfectly."

I know Libby's right. It's not like I'd substitute another skill during a softball game. When I was learning how to bunt, Mom pitched ball after ball to me until I got it. It was boring and it took hours, but it worked. This will work, too.

Eventually.

I flub another cartwheel.

"Let's do the big finish!" Libby exclaims. "We're good at that!"

Libby and I strike the final pose, then give each other a high five. My breath is coming in gasps, just like when I sprint to home base; and my heart feels as giddy as when I score a run. It's weird—I never thought that anything but softball could give me this high, but the more I think about performing in the talent show, the more excited I get.

Yeah, I'm still nervous, but not about performing. I'm nervous because we have to be good enough to win—to beat all the drummers and magicians and gymnasts who enter alongside us. That's why we need to keep practicing. Even on softball days, when we're already tired.

"One more time through." Libby looks at her phone. "If I don't get home by six o'clock, Mom's going to kill me."

"You could have dinner here." I fiddle with my bracelet. "I mean, if you want to. We only have frozen pizza and cereal, but it could be fun."

I don't want Libby to leave. I don't want to sit at home, in my room or in front of the TV, while Dad sells hammers and Mom discusses her *feelings* in some big building far away from me. I know why they have to be gone, but that doesn't change the fact that I've been alone a lot lately. Alone in my head and alone in my house. It's nice to finally have someone here alongside me.

"I do love cereal. Especially the sugary ones my mom never lets us buy. But I should go," Libby says. "We always have family dinners on Sunday nights. It's one of the things that's supposed to help Mom's 'recovery.'" She puts her fingers up in air quotes.

I frown at the unhappy expression on her face. "Is your mom okay?"

"Yeah," Libby says quickly, then bites her lip. "It's just . . . all this family togetherness makes me worry. Like the happiness is way too over-the-top and it's all just a big act until everything falls apart again."

"Maybe it's not an act," I say softly. "Maybe she really is getting better. Like my mom is." *I hope*, I add to myself.

Libby picks at her thumbnail, then looks up at me. "Mom has seemed weird lately. Tired. Not like herself. Kind of like she used to act sometimes . . ." She trails off. "I haven't smelled anything on her, but it still makes me worried."

"Did you tell your dad?"

"No. It's probably nothing."

"Right. Nothing."

We're both quiet for a few minutes. Is this what it's going to be like when *my* mom leaves rehab? Will I be worried forever, too? Analyzing everything she says and does?

Will life ever get back to normal?

"I'll talk to the support group about it at the next meeting," Libby says. "That'll help." She looks at me hopefully. "Can you come on Tuesday?"

I shake my head. "Maybe next time." It's one thing to talk to Libby, but I still can't imagine telling a whole group of strangers about my problems. Libby looks disappointed, so I keep talking. "Really. I'll try to go soon. I'm just balancing a lot right now. This *and* tryouts!"

"Me too." Libby looks down at the floor. "Do you really think I'll be able to perform in front of a whole crowd?"

"Absolutely!" I pat her on the shoulder, feeling like Coach Robertson hyping me up before I get up to bat. "You'll do fine."

"And you'll do great at tryouts," Libby says. "I promise. We'll both make the team, then we'll win the talent show. Where we'll sing. On stage. In front of people who could totally laugh at—"

I reach out and squeeze her hand. Libby's turning a strange shade of green. "I get it. Really. I feel like I'm going to barf whenever I see Coach Ortiz. I get so nervous that everything I do is stinktastic."

Libby rolls her eyes. "You're not stinktastic."

"I'm not as good as you."

The old Libby, the one I only knew from rec leagues games and the hallway at school, would have said something about how I'm totally right. How *no one* is as good as she is.

This Libby looks thoughtful, though. "Maybe not," she says. "But that's not a bad thing. Look at all the other stuff you can do. That *we* can do," she adds after a second.

I strike the final pose of our dance routine again, and Libby laughs, then heads for the door. "Keep practicing, okay?"

"We have to." I point to the calendar on my wall. "The talent show is only a few weeks away and softball try-outs are in just over a week." My head spins just thinking about everything I have to do—and do just right—but I push my worries aside. I'll take it step by step, day by day.

Just like Mom is doing.

"We've got this."

I give Libby a high five, and she makes her arms into big muscles. "We're superheroes!"

I mimic her, pretending that I'm wearing a cape and soaring over the city. Over my house and my middle school and even Pine Knolls, so that the building and the beautiful green lawn and Mom and her problems are small and solvable beneath me.

Twenty-Seven

Dear Mom,

I started this letter about a billion times. I wrote about how much I miss you. Then I wrote about how I was fine without you.

I wrote about how awesome things are at home. Then I wrote about how messy the kitchen is and how sick I am of peanut butter sandwiches for lunch and pizza for dinner. (We've tried different toppings to mix it up, but I still could live without seeing cheese again for a long time. And let me tell you—anchovies 100% taste as gross as they look.)

I wrote about how I'm rocking softball. Then I wrote about how the All-Star team is the best and maybe even the worst thing that's happening to me.

I miss you, Mom. I even miss you yelling at me to get up in the morning. I miss you telling me that I can't have ice cream for breakfast and that if I miss the bus, I'll have to walk to school backward.

I was angry at you for a long time. I think a little bit (okay, a lot) of me is still angry. I still don't all the way understand how this is a disease. It's not hard to make a decision—can't you decide to drink water instead of wine? Just like I decide to drink pink lemonade instead of iced tea?

Your brain is sick and it yells at you, though. That's what Dad says. I'm trying to believe him. I'm trying to believe you. To believe in you like you believe in me.

Softball tryouts are soon and I'm super scared. I might erase this part of the letter later. Because even though you guys always say it's brave to be scared and do something anyway, I still don't like being scared. Part of me doesn't want to try out at all.

Does that make me the opposite of brave?

I'm glad I can write to you now. Sometimes I imagine you talking to me when I have questions about stuff. Like how to cook scrambled eggs. (Dad always burns them.) Or where my stationery is. (I'm sorry this letter is on boring old paper. I hope it looks nice enough for you.) Do you ever imagine my voice? Are you forgetting it at all? (I wish I could include a recording of my voice. Except I always sound weird in recordings.)

I do know that you wouldn't forget me. It's a scary thought, though, because sometimes it felt like you forgot me and Dad. Like drinking was more important than us.

I shouldn't have written that. I should cross that out, too. Dad said this letter should be happy, but I've filled it with stuff that's going to stress you out. I want to tell you the truth, though. I want you to know how I feel so we can fix it.

I haven't been telling the truth to other people. Am I supposed to tell them where you are? Is this a forever secret?

I have a lot of questions, Mommy. I guess my biggest ones are: What do I do now? What happens when you come home? When can I see you? Should I see you?

Those are a lot of big questions.

I wonder if you're just as confused as me.

I love you,
Veronica

I wrote it.
I mailed it.
Then I totally freaked out.

Twenty-Eight

O f course I wake up with a stomachache the day of tryouts. It's not *that* bad, but I know it could make me slower. It could stop me from playing at full Veronica power. My warm-up run is slower than usual, too. Even though Claudia *tells* me I look smooth and powerful, I can tell that Coach Ortiz is watching me the entire time, wondering why someone as awful as me has the nerve to try out for the All-Star team.

Maybe she isn't watching me, though. Maybe I'm just imagining those bug-eyed sunglasses tracking my every move, like they're equipped with some superpowered radar.

Either way, is this what the *entire* season is going to be like? Feeling the pressure build up in my stomach until it literally twists itself into knots?

I head over to the dugout for my first station and pick up a bat, then swing fiercely, pretending I'm whacking this entire situation into the outfield. My heart feels like it's split in half, with one chamber wanting nothing more than to make the team and the other chamber wishing that there wasn't an All-Star team at all, that I could just go back to playing softball for fun and not having to worry about scouts and coaches and high-pressure tournaments.

But whatever happens, I'm here now. I'm going to do the best I can, because I do want to find out if all my hard work over the past few years has paid off. I need to know if me playing on this team is the fix that Mom needs.

"I'm exhausted!" Claudia comes up beside me after my first two at-bats, her face bright red. She's been across the grass, fielding the ground balls that Coach Ortiz's assistant has been hitting to a bunch of kids. I kept peeking over at Claudia to see how she was doing. We've both been so busy lately, and it's strange to not know how she's doing, both in softball and in life. It's not like we've been ignoring each other, but since that last conversation on the phone— and my decision to not tell her about the talent show—it's been weird between us.

We talk, but about boring stuff, like school and the weather. Which are things Dad and Mom would chat about with people they run into at the grocery store, not what I should talk to my best friend about. Every time we get close, though, even if we're alone, it doesn't seem to go any further than that. It's like we're digging a hole, but when we put our shovels in the dirt, there's a layer of rock under there, preventing us from going any deeper.

"I'm tired, too." I pull at the neck of my jersey and wipe away the sweat. (Apparently I can't get through that rock today, either.) "You're doing great." I point back to the ground ball area. "You fielded every one."

"*Almost* every one." Claudia wrinkles her nose. "The sun got into my eyes once and I fumbled the ball. Stupid sun."

"Stupid sun," I agree, then yell at myself. Stop talking about the weather! I lean forward and stretch my right hamstring, which is sore from all the dancing Libby and I have been doing. Which reminds me that I need to tell Claudia about the talent show. I'm going to sign Libby and myself up tonight, so there's no way I can hide the news for much longer.

I need to tell her about Mom, too. *And* about why I've waited so long to tell her everything that's been going on.

I shake my head. How did everything get so tangled up?

"Veronica Conway, you're next!" Coach Ortiz yells from across the field. I cringe. She's really loud.

"My turn," I say unnecessarily.

"Good luck!" Claudia's voice is cheerful, but her eyes don't have the spark they usually do when we're together, the one that's kindled by our shared past—by memories of baking mint, peanut butter, and raspberry brownies (sounds gross, tastes awesome) at sleepovers, protecting our shared secret that we're both afraid of Ferris wheels, and having marathon Mario Kart races.

"Thanks!" I try to make my smile all sparkarific, like I'm one big firework. I try to show Claudia with that one word that things *can* be okay between us again, that even though I'm not sure what to say about her parents, even though I'm not *letting* her figure out what to say about *my* mom, that we're still Veronica and Claudia, best friends forever.

The firework splutters, though. All I get from Claudia is a fist bump and an awkward smile. Which is okay. We're not going to be back to normal right away. It'll take time.

And honesty. I try to push that thought out of my head, though, and step up to the plate. I take a few practice swings, then stare at the pitcher, a girl named Millie who was on another one of the rec teams. She's been doing awesome so far. So good that I bet she'll make the team. Millie still has some tells, though. I can tell that when she's about to throw a fastball, she looks at the dugout first. She whips her arm back a bit differently when she throws a curveball, too.

The first pitch is too wide, and I don't swing.

"Ball!" Coach Ortiz shouts.

I swing at the second pitch, which I can tell is going to be a curveball. I hit the ball to the left of the third base line, though, which counts as my first strike.

But I felt strong. I made good contact. I know I can get a hit from Millie.

That's when I notice Coach Ortiz staring at me—so intently she's barely blinking. My heart feels like it's been stopped by some supervillain's freezing ray.

"Veronica?" Millie shouts from the pitcher's mound. "You ready?"

I nod and immediately go back into my batting stance. It's a good thing I'm wearing a helmet, because I bet my cheeks are bright red. A pitcher wouldn't ask me if I was ready during a game. I would have been caught totally off guard, and Coach Ortiz knows that.

The pitch speeds over the plate, but I'm too distracted to make contact.

"Strike two!"

Gah! Why is my brain sabotaging me like this? Coach Ortiz is going to be watching me all day long today—all *season* long—so I'd better get used to it.

"Come on, Veronica!" Claudia shouts from the sidelines. My heart leaps. Maybe things *can* be okay between us again . . .

I shake my head and grip my bat more tightly. I'll worry about Claudia later. Right now, I need to stay focused. Millie's next ball goes wide, and even though I want to hit it—want to hit a home run and show everyone that I can do this—I hold back.

Which was totally the right decision.

"Ball two!"

It's a two and two count, and my knees are shaking. I take a deep breath and give myself a pep talk. *You can do this. You're a softball player. You want this. You thrive under pressure.*

That's the thing, though—I *don't* thrive under pressure. And the more pressure that gets piled on, the more I wonder if I actually *do* want this.

No. I shake my head. *Of course* I want this. I've been watching the All-Star girls for years now, sitting in the stands and dreaming of wearing that awesome uniform with the star on the back. It's what Mom and I dreamed of, for me to be as good a player as she was. As Grandma Kathy was. As Great-Grandma Rose was.

I keep getting distracted, though, thinking about the lyrics of our talent show song and how to better harmonize with Libby.

I force my attention back to the action. *You got this, Veronica. Hit it hard.*

Millie swings her arm backward and releases the ball, and my eyes follow it as it travels toward me. I read an article once about some guy who had a near-death experience. He described how time slowed down and his life flashed before his eyes. I'm not having flashes of myself as a baby or anything, but it does feel like time has been set to slow-motion.

I grip the bat tighter, not sure whether I'm wishing for a hit or a whiff. I hear the sharp crack of the bat and feel the satisfying thud as I make contact. Before I can even think about it, my feet propel me up the first-base line.

In a game, I'd be making mental calculations the entire time. Did someone catch the ball? Should I try for another base? This is only the first day of tryouts, though, so all I do is run past first base, then trail to a stop and turn around. My breath comes in gasps, and I immediately search out Coach Ortiz.

She's already concentrating on Cara Dunbar, who's up next.

I'm not sure what I wanted from Coach Ortiz—a compliment? A pat on the back? It was just a hit, after all.

"Nice work!" Claudia runs over and gives me a high five. "You nailed that one!"

I grin. Best friends—even if they have been distant lately—always come through. "Thanks!" I grab my water bottle and take a gulp. "I was super nervous." I decide to try to break through that layer of rock.

"Me too!" Claudia exclaims. "I feel like I'm on one of those reality shows, with cameras recording my every move."

I snort. "Does that mean that if we make the team, Coach Ortiz will give us a rose?"

Claudia giggles. "It'd smell way better than our gym bags."

I put my bat in the pile by the dugout and start heading over behind home plate, where we're taking a water break before our end-of-tryouts scrimmage. It'll be our chance to show the coaches how we can play in a game-time situation—the most important part of today. The scariest part of today, too.

I made it through the beginning of tryouts, though. Which means I can totally rock the scrimmage.

And do something else that's scary.

After tryouts, I'm going to tell Claudia everything. I jog toward Claudia, then stop when I feel a hand on my shoulder.

"Nice work today!" Libby's face and uniform are streaked with dirt ("softball makeup," we call it), and I give her a high five.

"You too!" I'd been peeking at Libby during tryouts and she crushed the ball a bunch of times.

Claudia looks back at me and Libby, her eyebrows arching up in surprise. "Are you guys . . . friends?" She waves to Tabitha and Lauren, who join the rest of the girls by our pile of water bottles.

Libby smiles at Claudia like nothing at all weird is going on. Which, to her, is true. "Of course we are!" Her smile gets bigger as she strikes a pose. "Didn't Veronica tell you about our amazing talent show routine?"

The words emerge from Libby's mouth as if someone pressed the SLOW MOTION button. I want to jump forward and grab them before they hit Claudia's ears. I want to turn back the clock and give myself one more minute—one more second, even—to tell Claudia myself.

To prevent the hurt look that's already spreading across Claudia's face.

"Talent show?" she asks. "You guys are doing the talent show?"

"Yeah." I look down at my mud-covered cleats as the rest of the girls start to find their positions on the field around us. "It's not a big deal, though. Really. We're just singing and dancing."

"To our favorite song!" Libby hums a few bars.

"You mean the song *we* sing and dance to?" Claudia takes a step backward.

"Um, yeah. But it's not a big deal." I say the words quickly. "Really. I just forgot to tell you."

"I didn't mean to take over something that was yours!" Libby's face looks stricken. "I was just trying to help Veronica raise money for the softball fees, since rehab is so expensive." She leans toward Claudia confidingly, like *of course* Claudia knows what's going on.

Anyone would *assume* Claudia would know, after all.

But she doesn't.

I want to scream at Libby that she promised not to tell anyone. That she's a huge tattletale traitor. But deep down, I know that Libby didn't think she was doing anything wrong. She didn't know that because of her words, the world is now closing in on me, spinning in ever-tightening circles until I feel like my entire body is about to implode.

"Rehab?" Claudia says the word softly, like she's not sure what it means.

"Yeah. For her mom . . ." Libby's eyes widen, and she turns to me as Claudia's face falls. "You didn't tell her?" she whispers.

"You didn't tell me *what*? Veronica might not be able to play?" Claudia's head whips back and forth between me and Libby. "What's going on?"

I look down at the ground and wish that a sinkhole would open up in the middle of the field and swallow me whole. I *knew* I should have told Claudia the truth.

"Yeah." I can't bring myself to look up. "I might not be able to play on the All-Star Team."

"Why are you at tryouts, then?" Claudia asks. "And

you're just telling me this *now*? What's going on with your mom? Is she sick?" She sounds worried, which makes me feel even worse. *Of course* Claudia cares about my mom. Of course she's not judging me.

"I messed up," I say miserably. "I'm sorry."

Libby's head whips back and forth between us. "Uh, maybe I should go?"

"No!" I snap, then immediately shoot Libby an apologetic glance. "I'm sorry. You didn't do anything wrong."

Claudia blinks a bunch of times, like she's trying to hold back tears. "Why didn't you tell me about the talent show, either, Veronica? Do you not trust me?"

"I do!" I pause, realizing that I'm doing exactly what Mom used to do, when she told us that everything was fine and when it totally wasn't. When her lying ruined so much about our family.

"No." Claudia fixes me with a laser beam stare. "You don't."

Then she runs to meet the rest of the players, leaving me in the dirt without a chance to explain.

Without the words to explain, either.

Twenty-Nine

When I get home from tryouts, there's a letter on the table with my name on it.

Veronica Conway.

The return address says it's from Pine Knolls and the handwriting is one hundred percent, abso-total-lutely Mom's.

All of these clues add up in my mind, but the pieces click together slowly, like a snail is solving the puzzle. I picture a snail in one of those detective hats, with the wide brim all around, holding a mini magnifying glass and notebook. Usually, the thought of something like that would make me smile, but not today.

Today I'm too sad, and all I can do is stare at the envelope I'm about to open.

I *should* open it, right? That's why I wrote Mom a letter in the first place. To hear how she's doing. I won't be able to know that unless I open the envelope.

My fingers slowly make their way toward the flap. It's sealed with tape, which makes me smile the teensiest bit.

Mom always says that envelope glue is her least favorite taste in the whole world, worse than even liver and onions or that gross prune juice she gives me when I have . . . uh . . . stomach issues. If she can't find a sponge, she always tapes the back of the envelope, then pops a sticker on top, usually from a huge sheet of multicolored hearts she keeps in the junk drawer.

There's no sticker on this envelope, but there *is* tape. Which makes me think that the real Mom is still out there somewhere, quirks and all. That if part of her is on the *outside* of this envelope, then part of her must be on the inside, too.

That there could be good news in there.

"What if there isn't, though?" I whisper to myself.

I remember one time a few years ago when I overheard Dad mention something called "Schrödinger's cat" to Mom. At first, I'd thought he and Mom had *finally* conceded to my years-long battle for a kitten. It turns out that Dad was talking about some concept in a book he was reading.

Apparently some philosopher came up with this idea that if there's a box, you have no idea if there's a cat in it or not. And until you open up that box, both options are possible. So it's basically like there both is and isn't a cat . . . at the same time!

It didn't make much sense to me then. I'd just whined at my parents that if there was *always* a cat in the box, it'd have way more fun living with us.

Now, though, I get it. Today, I have my very own Schrödinger's letter. If I open it up, I might get bad news about Mom. But if I leave it closed, the good news will never disappear. It will always be there.

Buzz!

I look down at my phone as it vibrates with a text from Dad, relieved to take a momentary break from this potentially life-changing decision.

At the hardware store until eight. There's money beside the stove for dinner.

Yay. More pizza. I grimace, then check the time. It's six o'clock, but I'm not hungry. Apparently losing your best friend can mess with your appetite. I look around the kitchen, trying to figure out how to distract myself so I don't think about the words floating around inside that envelope. I'm not in a TV mood and I finished my last library book last night. I don't even have any homework this weekend! I could practice, but even hearing music makes me think of Claudia.

I wonder if she's thinking about me.

I try to read a book, but I can't concentrate, even though it's super good. I turn on the TV, but Netflix isn't connecting.

"Of course!" I throw up my hands and flop back against the couch, then head into the kitchen for a snack. I can't deal with pizza again, but I need something to quiet my rumbling stomach. I grab an apple and some peanut butter, then sit at the kitchen table, the sealed envelope in front of me.

I think about when I was a kid and I used to pick dai-
sies in the backyard. *He loves me, he loves me not. He loves*
me, he loves me not. I'd pick petals off and imagine that if I
ended on "he loves me," I'd grow up to marry Flynn Rider
from *Tangled.*

I de-petal an imaginary daisy in my mind. *Open the*
letter, leave it sealed. Open the letter, leave it sealed . . .

I hold it up and rotate it before my eyes, trying to see
if the envelope is see-through. Maybe if I can see a word
or two, I'll be able to tell if it's good news. The envelope is
thick, though. Nothing shows through.

I take an apple slice and dip it in peanut butter, then
chew really slowly. I'll open it when I finish this slice.

No, the next slice.

When the whole apple is gone, I stare at the letter, my
heart pounding out of my chest. The closest thing I have
to Mom is inside. It makes me angry—I *should* have the
real Mom here. But it also makes me grateful. At least
Mom can write to me. At least she's healthy.

I hope.

I think.

I guess it's time to find out.

Dear Veronica,

I miss you, too. I miss you more than words can say. I'm
going to try, though, because right now, words are all I

have. *The written word is hard. There's so much pressure for me to craft the perfect message here. On the phone I could just start talking. I'd plan beforehand, of course, but there'd be no way for me to go back over my words again, to edit and delete and rewrite them until they're perfect. In person, I could just hug you, and hope that my touch is able to communicate all the love and regret in my heart.*

Here, I have to stare at my words as I write them. I have to know that once your eyes are on this letter, I can't explain exactly what I mean or clarify some small detail. You can't hear my tone. The letters, the words, the sentences . . . they're all here, unchanging.

I need to realize that I can't change the past, though. Once I write this letter, it's done. I can't alter it, just like I can't alter the things that I did to hurt our family. To hurt you.

I'm so sorry that I wasn't the mother you needed me to be. I've been learning in here that I need to make amends for the things I did wrong, but that I also can't excuse them away. I messed up. I hurt you. And I am so, so sorry.

I know that you'll never understand how I valued drinking so much. I still don't understand it myself. I don't understand how a bottle . . . a glass . . . a few sips of liquid pulled me away from the love that you and your father gave me every day.

I could say that there's something in my brain that made me vulnerable to this addiction. I could say that that same brain told me to drink and that it was hard to disobey that voice in my head.

I could say that. It would be the truth, too.

It would also be an excuse. I don't want to lean on excuses anymore. I want to move forward and make changes.

I'll always be an alcoholic, Veronica. I may battle this disease forever. But I promise you with all of me—with every heartbeat of love I have for you—that I will fight this disease forever. I will not take another sip of alcohol because each sip takes me away from you.

Being your mother is the great privilege, honor, and gift of my life. I treasure it more with every day, especially since I almost lost it. I pray that I haven't lost it and that you haven't given up on me.

I love you so much, honey, and I'm so proud of you. Whether or not you make the softball team. Whether you play softball or choose something else entirely to love.

Family Day is next weekend and I would love if you and your Dad would come. I've sent him a letter, too.

> *My love always,*
> *Mom*

Thirty

"So you signed us up?" Libby throws me the softball and I easily catch it. We're on the school fields after school, even though there's no practice today. Rec league is over for the year—Libby's team beat ours in the final game of the season—and we have to wait a few more days until we even find out if we've made the All-Star team.

Usually, I'd be hanging out with Claudia. We'd paint our nails in her room or have Netflix marathons. We'd ride our bikes to the store in the center and get ice cream cones, then take the long way home to avoid doing our homework.

Claudia's ignoring me, though. I don't know if that means we're in a fight or she's not my friend anymore. We never sat down and decided what's going on. She just stormed off the field after tryouts and hasn't talked to me since. Tabitha and Lauren are so confused that they're avoiding us entirely.

So I'm with Libby instead. Which isn't a bad thing. I just feel weird, like there's a part of me missing.

"Yep." I toss the ball back at Libby. "I just made the deadline, too."

"Whew!" Libby mimes wiping a bead of sweat off her forehead. "You mean we almost *didn't* have to get on stage and totally and completely embarrass ourselves?"

"Libby." I motion for her to hang on to the ball, then move across the field toward her. "Are you sure you're okay doing this? I can do it alone. I just . . . well, I thought it'd be fun to do together."

Especially now that I don't have any other friends left.

"Nah, I'm just nervous." Libby tosses the softball between her hands. "I'll be okay. As long as I don't eat anything before the show." She puffs out her cheeks like she's going to barf.

"Eww!" I giggle. "And good. Because they didn't have any more spots for solo acts, so I need a partner!" I take my glove off my sweaty hand and wipe it on my pants. "I really think we can win that prize."

"Then we can hang out even more this summer!" Libby smiles. "As long as we both make the team. Which we will. Totally."

I raise my eyebrows at her. "You'll make it for sure. *You* did amazing." I think back on the tryouts and all the mistakes I made. "You didn't drop three fly balls and almost strike out."

There's been a pit in my stomach ever since tryouts,

and not just because of Claudia. I can't stop thinking about how much better all the other girls did than me. About how much tougher All-Star games will be. What if I make the same mistakes then? What if the pressure gets to me? My chest tightens just thinking about it.

"You did awesome!" Libby says. "Seriously."

"I'm super nervous," I admit.

"You'll be fine." Libby's voice is light. "You love softball. Just focus on having fun."

Was it fun, though? *Is* it fun? I don't know anymore.

I hold out my arm. "Look at how much my hand is shaking. Every time I think about the team, my body turns into Jell-O."

Libby giggles. "What flavor?"

"Anything but lime." I smile. "Because lime . . ."

Libby doesn't say anything, though. She tilts her head to the side quizzically as I finish the sentence in my head.

Because lime tastes like slime.

It's from the time in third grade when Claudia and I did a science project ranking the flavors of freeze pops. It was a *super*-technical process involving lots of freeze-pop eating. Lots and lots. Blue raspberry and strawberry tied for first, but no matter which brand we tried, lime always lost.

It's always been one of my favorite memories, and usually makes my insides feel happy.

Today it makes my stomach churn.

Libby may be my new friend. She may understand

what it's like to have an alcoholic mom, too. But she's not Claudia.

I miss Claudia. I may not have *directly* lied to her, but I didn't tell her the whole truth. *Any* of the truth, actually.

I think about how even though I know Dad got a letter from Mom about Family Day, he still hasn't mentioned it to me yet. He's doing that "Dad thing" where he keeps hinting around something without actually mentioning it.

Like talking about how nice it was to hear from Mom and "boy, wouldn't it be nice to see her in person?"

Like mentioning how Mom misses me and how pretty Pine Knolls is.

Like leaving out all these articles about how important therapy is and how my generation is "way savvier" about mental health than his. ("The Savvy Schoolkids"—that was the actual name of one of the articles. Insert eye roll here.)

I know he's trying to get *me* to bring up Family Day so he can claim that it's my idea. He did the same thing when my distant cousin Erin got married last year in some small town in Florida in the middle of August and he kept talking about how pretty Florida was in the summer.

Which, duh, Dad, that's prime hurricane season, but of course he didn't think of that. Instead, he wanted me to *ask* to go to Florida, which would make him feel less guilty about dragging our whole family on a road trip to Boringtown, USA, where we might be in mortal weather danger.

I didn't take the bait, and luckily Mom backed me up. We sent a card and an ugly vase instead.

But the whole Florida drama took almost five whole days to figure out, all because Dad didn't want to have a hard conversation.

He's doing the same thing now, and I am *not* here for it. If he wants me to go to Family Day, the least he can do is tell me that he wants me to go to Family Day. Even Mom was direct with me, if only in letter form.

That's why I've been ignoring the hints and the strategically placed articles. Why I'm waiting for Dad to actually talk to me like a normal adult. Maybe Mom got so bad because Dad couldn't confront her earlier. Maybe if he'd spoken up, she'd still be here right now.

I don't know if that's the answer to Mom's alcoholism, any more than me making the All-Star team. The more time that passes, the more I'm starting to think that there may not be one answer at all.

But I deserve more than silence. Now more than ever.

Claudia deserves more than that, too.

Thirty-One

"I made it." I blink, like my action will somehow make the words on the page disappear. That Coach Ortiz used some sort of magic ink to torture the girls who didn't make the team.

But no. There's my name up there:

Veronica Conway.

Libby's name is right below mine. Claudia and Tabitha made the team, too.

"No!" Next to me, Lauren's eyes widen in shock. She turns to me. "I . . . didn't make it." Her voice is wooden, like she left all her emotions *and* energy on the field.

I reach out to give her a hug, but she pulls away. "I . . . need to go." Her sobs trail behind her as she runs down the hallway, and I move to follow her, but Tabitha puts her hand on my arm. "It's okay," she says, her face a mix of excitement and sadness. "I got her."

I watch Tabitha trail Lauren, then look at the list again. I feel the same way, only for a different reason. *Of course*

I'm excited I made the team. I've been waiting for this list to go up for days. Years, even, if you count the first All-Star game I went to when I was eight, when I stood on the third-base line, my fingers curled around the chain-link fence, my eyes wide open.

Of course I'm excited, I repeat to myself.

Then why do I keep checking the list, wishing that my name wasn't up there?

"We did it!" Libby bounds up next to me and gives me a hug, and I push the traitorous thoughts away. That's what they are, after all. I'm a softball player, which means I play softball. Coach Ortiz herself decided I was good enough.

"We did!" I force some energy into my voice and hug her back. "It'll be so much fun!"

"Totally." Libby leans closer to whisper in my ear. "This means that after the talent show this weekend, everything will be fine. Back to normal."

I pull away at the word *normal* and stare at the list again. *Normal* would be my mom being home. *Normal* would be my mom never going away in the first place. But in a way, Libby's right—playing softball is as normal as things can get right now. I force another smile and turn back to her. "Absolutely."

"Sharing secrets again?" Claudia's voice comes from behind us, and I whirl around to face her.

"No! Really. I promise." My words come out so fast that they sound insincere and rehearsed, and I take a deep breath. "We weren't sharing any secrets, Claudia."

She's not looking at me, though, and I follow her eyes to the list. "Congratulations," I say softly. "You did awesome at tryouts."

"You too," Claudia finally says. She sounds like a kid forced to be polite, but I'll take what I can get.

"Claudia, I—"

She shakes her head and cuts me off. "Veronica, don't. I . . . I don't know why you didn't tell me the truth about what's going on. I don't even know exactly *what's* going on, but I do know that you don't trust me. And that hurts. A lot."

Tears prick at my eyes and I nod furiously. "I know. I really do. And I get why you're mad. I just . . . can we talk? So I can explain?"

Claudia moves to let a few other kids look at the list. Her face hasn't changed expression at all. I feel like I'm back at our kitchen table, when my parents explained Mom's alcoholism. Except now the places have changed—now *I'm* the one listing all the ways I've messed up.

"Please." I clasp my hands together. I probably look silly and everyone is probably watching, but I don't care. I want my best friend back.

Claudia sighs loudly. "Fine."

My eyes light up.

"Later, though." She looks up at the clock, which is about to ring for first period. "After school."

"I can wait."

And I can. I think back to the kitchen table again, about all this time that Mom's been gone.

I've learned to do that, at least.

~~~~~~~~~~~~~~~~~~

"I have been keeping secrets from you." Claudia and I are sitting in my backyard, her on the tire swing, me on the ground beneath it. It's sunny and warm and the sky is a clear blue, but inside, I feel full of dark clouds.

"And you told them to Libby instead?" Claudia's voice is shaky. "I'm your best friend, Veronica."

"I know." I pluck a blade of grass from the lawn, then force myself to meet Claudia's eyes. "I didn't tell you for a reason, though. I know you've been sad about your parents and I didn't want to stress you out even more."

"You keeping *secrets* stresses me out." Claudia pushes off the ground, setting the tire swing twirling in a circle. I watch her spin, my own head whirling even faster. "And that's . . . well, it's a dumb reason not to tell me. I'd rather be *more* stressed out than be totally in the dark."

I imagine Claudia and me stumbling through a darkened room, reaching out for each other and banging into things. It's exactly the way I've been feeling lately, at home *and* with her.

"Lights are good," I admit.

I think Claudia cracks a smile, but by the time the tire spins back around, the smile's gone again. "Yeah. And secrets are bad."

"I know." My nose does that "I'm totally going to cry" tingly thing, but I don't try to hold back the tears. I've been holding back too much lately.

"Mom isn't on a business trip." The first words are hard to get out, but once the dam is breached, the rest of them flow out like roaring floodwaters. "She's in rehab and she's been drinking too much and she's an alcoholic and I was afraid that if I told you you'd worry or look at me weird or think Mom was messed up or *I* was messed up and . . . and . . . I might not get to do softball because Mom and Dad are all stressed and they'll be too busy to bring me and it costs money and I don't know what I even want to do . . ." I break off, my breath coming in gasps.

Claudia reaches down and squeezes my hand. "I'm so sorry, Veronica."

I squeeze back. "Thanks." I look up at Claudia hopefully, but that's all she says. "Are you still mad?" I ask.

Claudia sighs, then stops the tire swing and finally looks me in the eye. "Yes. No. Kind of? I'm just sad, I guess. And confused? Why didn't you trust me?"

"I did trust you, though! I do!" I want to hug Claudia, but I can't risk doing anything that could make things worse. (She's on a tire swing, too, so that'd be pretty awkward.) "I was just trying to make your life easier. And to be honest, I guess I was a little bit jealous."

"Jealous?"

"That your mom wants to spend so much time with

you. Meanwhile, mine's off at rehab and Dad's working nonstop. I miss them."

"I miss you," Claudia says. "And I wish I could have helped more."

"I miss you, too!" A tear drips down my face. "I miss everyone."

"Except Libby." Claudia bites her lip. "Is she your new best friend now?"

"No way!" I climb onto the tire swing next to Claudia, causing it to dip us both backward. I grip onto the chains. "She is my friend, though. She was easy to talk to."

I don't know how to tell Claudia that sometimes it's easier to share a life-altering secret with someone *besides* your best friend.

How, that way, you don't have to push through layers of childhood memories.

How starting off on a clean sheet of paper means that you don't have to find a clear space to write a new story on.

(I don't tell Claudia why Libby understands so well, though. That's not my secret to share, after all.)

"Oh."

"I didn't want you to worry." I try to catch Claudia's eye, but she's looking at the grass. At the sky. At a squirrel running by. Anywhere but at me, the worst best friend ever. "And I didn't want you to look at me any different. Remember how you said I'm Veronica with the perfect family?"

"Right. *That*." Claudia sighs.

"We're not perfect at all," I admit. "Dad's Mr. Cheerful half the time, Mom's not even here, and I'm . . ." I trail off. "I'm just angry. A lot."

"I guess maybe there's no such thing as a perfect family," Claudia says softly.

"Maybe not." My eyes follow a bird as it flits from tree to tree.

"Did you know that some people think birds bring good luck?" Claudia follows my gaze.

The bird finally settles down in a nest at the top of our old oak tree. "Grandma Helen told me that once," I say. "She said that a bird pooped on her head on her way to her wedding, and that it was actually a good-luck sign."

"Ew!" Claudia covers her head with her hands.

"Exactly." I giggle, then cover my mouth in horror. "Can you even imagine? I'd say it's the exact *opposite* of good luck. But Grandma said that she just wiped it off and went and got married. I guess it worked, because they never got divor—" I break off, my hands flying to my mouth. "Oh no. I shouldn't have said that."

Claudia waves her hand in the air. "It's okay. Really. My parents probably *are* going to get divorced, and no amount of bird poop is going to stop that from happening." Her words are sad, but there's a twinkle of something else—hope? acceptance?—in her eyes. "It's probably a good thing anyway."

"A good thing?" I say slowly.

"Yeah." Claudia grasps onto the chains and tilts her head back toward the sky. "You've heard them fight. It's awful."

"True." I remember going over to Claudia's house during winter vacation. We made friendship bracelets to the soundtrack of her parents yelling about her mom not refilling the car with gas and her dad not vacuuming the house enough. Claudia turned the music up so high to drown them out that I practically lost my hearing.

"It only got worse," she says.

"Yeah, I know." That's why we hung out at my house after that. Then at Tabitha's and Lauren's when I got so embarrassed about *my* mom that I didn't want anyone over, either.

"I saw a robin in the backyard one morning last winter, after they had a really big fight." I'm not sure what Claudia's point is, so I let her keep talking. "It was hopping around our garden, even though everything was all bare and wilted. There were leaves blowing all over the place, a bunch of dirt, and this little bird, just bopping along."

I smile at the idea of a bopping bird. I bet it loves music as much as I do.

"I went online to look up what robins eat and found this whole website about bird meanings. About how seeing a robin, especially in a garden, means that good luck will happen to the people who live there." Claudia grips the chains more tightly. "It made me think that Mom and Dad were going to stop fighting so much, that all I had to do was find enough robins and everything would fix itself. I found *so many* robins, but it never worked out."

She sniffles, and I reach out to touch her shoulder. "This really stinks."

I didn't know what to say to Claudia before. I didn't know what someone with separated parents would want to hear and I didn't want to make it worse. Now, though, I say what's in my heart. I say what I wanted to hear—what I *still* want to hear—from people. That when parents have problems that kids can't fix, it just plain stinks.

Claudia wipes her eyes but doesn't quite get one of the tears dripping down her right cheek. I reach out and get it for her.

"You didn't have to do that."

"I know," I say simply. "I wanted to. To make up for what a jerk I've been."

"You haven't been a jerk." Claudia takes a deep breath and wipes her face again. "You were scared."

"So were you," I say. "And I should have trusted that you'd be here for me. You've never given me any reason not to."

"What about that prank I played in fourth grade . . ." Claudia trails off, that same spark entering her eyes again.

I immediately know what she's talking about. "When you put glitter in every single pocket of my softball bag . . ."

"And when you opened it up, it got all over your mom's car?" Claudia is laughing so hard she almost topples over. "That was the best!"

"It was not!" I exclaim. "I got grounded for the whole weekend and it took ages for me to brush my hair without getting glitter all over the place." I giggle. "Mom said you were a bad influence on me."

Claudia bites her lip. "Maybe I am."

"What? No," I protest.

"Or at the very least, maybe I'm not a good friend." Claudia sniffles. "I wish I'd shown you that I could be trustworthy with the stuff about your mom."

"You did! I mean, you are." I take a deep breath and try to explain. "I think I just didn't want to change things with us. I didn't want to make you sadder or hurt our friendship with all this bad news."

"But your bad news is reality," Claudia says. "Same with the stuff about my parents. That's why I told you. Because I know that our friendship is strong enough to survive a little bit of sadness."

"Or a lot," I say.

"Or a lot."

"I'm sorry I kept Mom's alcoholism a secret." I say it as firmly as I can, and I look Claudia in the eyes. I need her to know how serious I am. "I know—I guess I *knew* all along—that you wouldn't judge her. Or me."

There's a teeny-tiny part of me that's still afraid that Claudia *will* judge me—that everyone in the world will—but I push it deep underground, under another layer of hard rock that no shovel will be able to penetrate.

"I'm sorry about the talent show, too. I didn't mean to

leave you out." I *kind* of did, but I don't tell her that part. "You can be in the act, too, if you—"

"No way!" Claudia laughs and shakes her head. "But I *will* be there cheering for you."

"Yay!" Having Claudia in the audience will make the show even better.

"Your mom is awesome." Claudia gives me a hug. "I'm glad she's getting better. I'm glad your family will be getting better."

"I don't know what's going to happen once Mom is home. Or what she's going to be like when I see her again." I say the words quietly. It's the first time I've spoken my fear out loud.

"She'll be different. You'll all be different. Just like my family will be."

"What if that stinks, too?" I ask.

"It might. But it might not." Claudia's voice is hopeful, but her eyes look worried. Maybe we'll both be worried for a long time. Maybe that's okay.

"But we'll get through it." I hug her back.

"Together."

Thirty-Two

"Fine." I walk into the family room and huff out a breath. "I'll go."

"Go?" Dad looks up from his show. He's been binging this high fantasy epic about dragons and warriors and half monster–half gods that's basically a bunch of people in armor constantly fighting. I tried to watch it with him once and was bored in like five seconds. I could barely see anyone's face, never mind hear the dialogue over the clashing of swords.

Dad's rapt, though, as usual. "Hold on a sec, Veronica." I thought he was going to pause. Wasn't my dramatic entrance dramatic enough? I even tossed my hair and pouted out my lip. He apparently didn't notice any of that, though, because he finishes out the scene, where a massive dragon breathes fire over an entire town, before clicking the TV off.

At least I have his full attention now.

"What's that?" he asks. "You'll go where?" He looks at

his watch. "It's late, honey. I don't want you out too long after dark."

I guiltily remember my midnight journey to the practice area in the park and force my face to look as innocent as possible. "I'll go see Mom," I announce. "For Family Day, I mean."

It's like my words have transformed Dad into another person, like he's an actor who showed up to a movie set with a bare face and messy hair and stepped out of the makeup trailer a glamorous superstar. "You will?" he breathes. "Oh, honey, I'm so glad. This will mean so much to your mother."

"I'm not doing it for her," I grump, although I'm not sure *who* I'm doing this for. Me? Claudia? My family? Whatever the reason, I know that I have to go.

"I'm just so glad you came to this decision—"

"Stop." I hold up a hand. "It wasn't all my decision and you know it."

Dad's cheeks get pink. Good. He *should* be embarrassed.

"I got all your hints. As usual." I shake my head. "Dad, you don't need to set up some mental gymnastics obstacle course to get my attention. I'm not a detective you have to clue in, either. You can just talk to me."

Dad fiddles with the buttons on the remote control, even though the TV is off. "I know." Channel up, channel down. Volume up, volume down. I better be careful the next time I turn the TV on.

"Do you?" I sit down next to Dad and put my hand on his arm. "I'm not going to get scared away by what's happening with Mom." I smile sadly. "There's nowhere to go. I have to deal with this because I love Mom. I love you. You guys are family, which means you're stuck with me."

It's the same with Claudia. We've been best friends for so long that she's basically like family. She's stuck with me, too. She loves me and she loves my mom. How could I have ever thought she'd think differently of me? Of us? How could *she* have worried the same thing about me?

Maybe deep down, we're all afraid of losing the things we love the most.

We don't have to be, though. Elastic bands may stretch and stretch until they snap, but we're not cheap elastic bands. We're not even bungee cords, which are strong enough to hold people when they jump off bridges. The bonds between people are thicker than that.

Especially the bonds between friends and family.

"I'm sorry I didn't ask you," Dad says finally. "I guess I have some things to work on, too, just like your mother does." His eyes brighten. "And hey! Family Day will be the perfect place to do that!"

"Okay . . . ," I say guardedly. "What's this whole day about anyway?"

"It'll be great!" Dad exclaims, and I honestly can't tell if he's genuinely excited or a totally optimistic fakerpants. "Family Day will help both of us," Dad continues. "We'll get to go to classes to learn all about your mother's illness, talk with other family members about what they're going through, and maybe see your mother's room."

"You're not exactly painting the prettiest picture," I say. I had imagined the three of us eating cookies and drinking lemonade together. Maybe they'd even have sports events, like they did at field day in elementary school. We'd play volleyball and have three-legged races. It'd be corny, but fun. We'd bond. "Will we get to do anything fun with Mom?"

"We'll get to have a meal with her," Dad say slowly. "And visit with her. We'll be doing a family therapy session together, too."

"Yippee."

"Veronica." Dad raises his eyebrows. "You *just* told me that I need to communicate."

That's you, *though*, I think to myself. It's something that we already *knew* you had trouble with. What if it turns out that *I'm* doing something that's messing up our family beyond repair? What if it's something I can't fix?

"What if I'm not good at therapy?" I whisper.

Dad puts his arm around me. He smells like sawdust and coffee. "It's impossible to be bad at therapy," he says softly. "You just need to talk and be honest."

"Libby said the same thing."

"Libby?"

"My new friend. Her mom's also an alcoholic, and she's been trying to get me to go to a support group. She made the All-Star team, too."

Dad blinks. "Well, that's a lot of information." He gives me a hug. "I'm glad that you two have each other. And I'm proud of you for making the team. I know you've been working really hard."

"I thought you said we can't afford it." Last time we had this conversation, I was a total grumpapotamus. Today, though, I'm not even mad. I know that Libby and I have a good chance at winning the talent show. And even if we don't . . . maybe not playing wouldn't be the worst thing in the world.

No.

Of course we'll win. Of course I'll be able to play. That's what this year has been all about, after all. Softball is what's always connected me and Mom before. If we lose that, it could ruin her recovery—and our bond—once she comes home.

"We're still figuring out what we can afford," Dad says evenly. "It's a conversation in progress."

I roll my eyes. "That's total dad-speak, you know."

"Well, I'm a dad, so that's what you're going to get." Dad ruffles my hair (which—ugh—he knows I hate). "We still have a few weeks to figure everything out before the season starts. But I *do* want you to know how proud I am. How proud Mom will be, too."

The thought makes me feel warm inside.

"I'm glad you want to go to Family Day," Dad says. "It'll help all of us, I promise. We'll get to talk about what life will be like when your mother gets home. What we can do to make things easier and how she can help us, too."

"Okay." It doesn't sound that bad, actually. Guidelines for Mom's homecoming will definitely help. Because even though we don't know *when* Mom is getting discharged, it suddenly hits me that she *will* be discharged. Pretty soon, Mom will be home. And even though that's all I've wished for lately, the thought scares me now.

What if Mom's *too* different?

What if she doesn't like it at home now that she doesn't drink?

What if I do something wrong?

Thirty-Three

It's sunny when I wake up on Family Day, even though the forecast had promised bucketfuls of rain. Even though the weathergirl on last night's news (the one who Dad says should have gone to drama school) wore a rain slicker, a yellow rain hat and boots during her forecast and did a little song and dance from Dad's favorite musical, *Singin' in the Rain.*

But when I open my eyes, sunshine streams through my windows. The birds are chirping, too, so loudly that I feel like I'm in the opening sequence of a cartoon. Soon they'll fly in here and help me get dressed. We'll sing a happy song and do a choreographed dance routine in the yard with the local bunnies and deer.

In reality, though, I roll out of bed with a *flump.* I *try* to do it gracefully, but my right leg gets caught in my sheets and I topple over sideways. I'm staring up at the ceiling, at the whirls and swirls of white, when Dad calls up to me.

"You okay up there, hon?"

I scramble to my feet and adjust the oversized Boston Red Sox t-shirt I wore to bed. It's two sizes too big so it always slides down over my shoulders. "Fine!" I shout back. "Just bumped into something."

Dad's footsteps pound closer to the door. "I was about to wake you up. I'm planning to leave in about half an hour, so you need to shower quickly. We don't have much in the house, so we can stop at Dunkin' on the way."

"Yum!" When I was a kid, Dad and I used to get doughnuts almost every Saturday morning, when Mom had to go into the office. He liked the maple frosted kind, and I loved the chocolate ones. Even better if they were chocolate with chocolate frosting and chocolate sprinkles.

I may not know exactly what's going to happen today, but at least it'll start off with a sugar rush.

I take a quick shower and change (I wear my favorite red-and-white-striped skirt, the one Mom says makes me look "so grown-up"), but when I go downstairs, Dad's not there. The light in his office is on, though, and when I peek inside, I see him in his work chair, staring at a picture of him and Mom on their wedding day.

I love looking at that picture. Mom and Dad got married on the beach, near the house in Cape Cod where Dad vacationed as a kid. They're standing right next to the water, Mom's train spread around her, the sand dunes spread before them. The sky is as blue as a robin's egg and there's not a cloud in the sky. If that wasn't enough of a good luck sign, the smiles on my parents' faces are as blinding as the sunshine beating down on them.

I wonder what Dad's thinking about.

I wonder if Mom drank a lot back then or if this is a new thing. I don't remember her drinking when I was a really little kid, but maybe she hid it back then. Maybe she hid it from Dad even further back.

"Are you mad still?" I've barely considered the words before they're out of my mouth.

Dad looks up from the picture, his eyes shimmering. I expect him to look sad, but his smile is bigger than I've seen in ages. "No."

"Not at all?" It seems unbelievable. Dad's been working two jobs, taking care of me, and worrying about Mom. Plus she lied to him. To us.

"Really," he says at my skeptical expression. "I *was* mad. I was Hulk-mad, even. But Holly helped me realize that I need to let go of that anger to move on. Which means that all I am right now is proud."

"Holly?" I ask.

"My therapist."

Of course. The mysterious therapist. "She really helped?" I ask. I still don't know if I want to talk to someone, but if it helped Dad this much, maybe it could help me, too. Maybe I can even start with Libby's support group. This week. I'll go this week for sure.

"So much." Dad tables his fingers together. "I'm not perfect. I have moments when I get so angry I could scream—"

"Me too!" I cut in.

"—but I try to push past those feelings. For the future," Dad says. "For all of us."

I guess that's what I can try to do, too.

Dad puts the wedding picture back, arranging it carefully so it sits exactly where it always does. "Should we go?" He stands and reaches out his hand to me.

"We should."

It's the truth, after all. It's time to move forward.

Thirty-Four

I wasn't sure what would happen when I saw Mom for the first time. When she saw *me*. I imagined some grand cinematic reunion, where the music (that would somehow be playing around us) would slow down and come to a dramatic crescendo. We'd rush at each other through the crowded entryway while everyone else froze in their tracks. She'd cry. I'd cry. We'd hug for some indeterminate time.

Then everything would be back to normal. We'd talk like normal and we'd laugh like normal. Normal, normal, normal.

In reality, though, our grand reunion is nothing like my daydream. We're not in the entryway; we're in a little room off a side hallway. It's cozy, with white walls and a few overstuffed chairs in a pretty blue-and-white print. There are a bunch of pictures that I bet are supposed to be calming—a sailboat, an apple orchard at sunset, and a flower garden filled with all the colors of the rainbow.

I hope they calm everyone here, because they're sure not working for me. Because the second Mom enters the room, my heart starts beating so fast I'm surprised it doesn't pop out of my chest like in some gross horror movie.

"Hi." Mom says the word softly, like I'm a baby kitten she's afraid to spook. She's still in the doorway, and Dad takes a step closer. He squeezes her hand, like he's infusing her with all the love she's been missing out on for the past month. Mom doesn't give him a hug or anything, though. She doesn't move at all—she's just focused on me.

I'm her priority. Not Dad. Not drinking. Not anything else in the whole wide world.

The thought makes my insides warm.

"Hi," I finally manage. I want to run to her and squeeze her tight, but I'm also afraid that I'll break her, that she's a statue made out of glass and anything I do wrong could be the hammer to shatter her. I take a small step closer. "Hi," I say again.

Mom sits down on one of the chairs and pats the cushions of the one next to her. I take it cautiously.

"I'm looking forward to today." She says it slowly and deliberately, like she's picking out apples in the grocery store, choosing the ones that are the brightest and least bruised.

"Me too."

"I wish I could spend more time with you two, but I have my own groups to go to." Mom brushes a strand of hair out of her eyes. For some reason, I'm surprised to notice that Mom's bangs are longer now. Of course Mom's hair would have grown in here. Lots of things about her are changing, after all.

I remember reading once that your skin cells replace themselves all the time, that we're always shedding old bits of dry skin and growing fresh new cells. It sounds kind of icky—who wants to think about all that gross skin falling off all the time?—but it's kind of comforting at the same time. That a month from now, there will be all new skin cells on the outsides of us.

Just like, in some amount of time, all of Mom's hair will be new. It'll be hair from the time when she isn't drinking anymore.

Not from when she was.

"Honey?"

I pull my gaze away from Mom's hair and finally meet her eyes. At least *they* look exactly the same.

"It's okay if you have groups," I manage. My eyes are filling up with tears and my throat feels thick with sobs. I told myself to be strong today, but my plan isn't exactly working. I take a deep breath, then puff it out as slowly and quietly as I can. "Dad told me that you're going to be busy with stuff."

"I have my therapist this morning and then a peer group. But we can have lunch together," Mom says. "And after lunch we'll meet as a family."

"We're so happy to be here, Anna." Dad finally wraps

Mom in a hug. I think about how when I was a kid, I always got super jealous whenever I saw my parents hugging. I'd run up and wrap my arms around one of their legs, then proclaim we were having a "hug party!"

Today, though, I let Mom and Dad have each other.

"We have some good news for you, too," Dad says once he's pulled away. His face is bright, his voice perky.

"Ooh, what?" Mom sounds the same way, like she's pretending to be the "Perfect Recovery Mom," someone who doesn't get upset about anything and whose life is going to be absolutely wonderful from now on.

I peer at Mom's face more closely. She actually *does* look a lot happier. Healthier, too—her cheeks are rosy and her eyes sparkle. Maybe she's *not* pretending—maybe Mom actually *is* doing well.

"Veronica?" Dad nudges me in the side.

"I made the All-Star team." I look at the ground when I say it. Well, whisper it, actually. Which is weird. You'd think I'd want to stand up on a table and shout it to the entire room. The entire world, even. Instead, I'm almost . . . embarrassed. Like I don't deserve to be on the team. Like this new bit of news is a puzzle piece that doesn't quite fit into the whole of me.

"Honey!" Mom screeches loud enough for all of us, though, then reaches forward and sweeps me up in a hug. "I'm so proud of you. You must have been working so hard without . . ." She pauses, a wistful expression passing across her face. "Well, without me."

"Mom, it's okay."

(I mean, it's *not* okay, but I can pretend to be Perfect Happy Daughter, too. That's half the point of today.)

"I'll make it up to you once I get out of here." Mom nods her head firmly. "You're going to have such a good season." She continues to gush as some Pine Knolls staff member starts to herd us into a different room.

As Mom's voice grows more animated, the pit in my stomach grows. Because seeing Mom so happy has made me realize that lately, *I* haven't been happy. That thinking about playing on the All-Star team *makes* me unhappy.

That as much as I've tried to deny it, I don't want to join the team at all.

Thirty-Five

"So is Family Day that bad?" Halfway through lunch, Dad leans over with one of those annoyingly smug Dad smiles on his face, the one he used after I insisted for years and years that I hated blueberries, then finally tried them and basically ate a quart a day for two months straight.

"No." I take another bite of my salad and avoid his eyes. A smile quirks at the side of my mouth, though, because I'm actually not annoyed that he's right. I'm happy that all my doubts were wrong, that this morning's informational session on alcoholism was pretty interesting. I felt like I was back in health class, but it was nice to learn that all the things Mom had been doing were part of an actual disease.

I mean, I did *already* know that. But hearing it from a professional, a guy with a name tag that said DOCTOR and a fancy bow tie, made it feel extra official.

We got a tour of Pine Knolls after that. I didn't get to

see Mom's room, which is part of a three-bedroom suite with two other women her age, but we did get to see a model apartment, with a common room, a television, and a kitchen where they cook their own meals.

"This reminds me of the dorm room I had senior year of college," Dad whispered to me. "Man, that place was party central. The kitchen was such a mess, too, always covered in empty beer bot—" He trails off, his eyes flitting to the woman giving the tour, like by just mentioning the word *beer* he'll get in trouble.

He might. Maybe he should. I think that's what we'll be talking about in our family session today—what Dad and I can do and say to help Mom after she leaves here. That, and what *she* can do to help our family get back on track.

I wonder if I *should* speak up about what Mom has done wrong. Will the therapist actually listen to me? Or will she think I'm a little kid and make Dad do the talking? What about softball? Mom and Dad keep saying how excited they are for me—is therapy the place to talk about how I feel?

No.

I can't.

Because every time I look at Mom, every time she squeezes my hand and tells me how excited she is to play catch with me again, my confidence wavers. I can't quit the team. We need to give Mom a stable home when she leaves Pine Knolls.

That's my job. My responsibility.

After we finish our catered lunch (rubbery chicken with sauce, shiny green beans, and a pretty yummy rice pilaf), Mom leads me and Dad to her therapist's office. We climb behind her to the third floor, to a room with a plaque outside reading DR. MONICA MARIA MARQUEZ, PHD, LICSW.

She sounds letter-tastically official. Alliterative, too.

Mom knocks on the door, and a clear, confident voice echoes out from inside.

"Come in!"

I wonder if you have to be super confident to be a therapist. I wonder if this M&M lady has any problems of her own. I wonder if she's judging us for being so messed up.

When I trail my parents inside, I look the therapist up and down. She seems normal. There's not even a couch inside, just a glass coffee table with pointy edges and a bunch of comfy chairs. I wonder if they buy the chairs in bulk here. The coffee table is covered with toys—there's a Rubik's Cube, a yo-yo, and one of those little square boxes with a sand garden inside. I reach over and use the little stick to trace a pattern before realizing that I could be doing something wrong. Already.

My head pops up. "I'm sorry." I pull my hand back.

"No worries at all." Monica's voice is deep and rich, like a hug wrapping the room in its warmth. "These things are here for you to do with as you wish. Right, Anna?" She shoots Mom a mischievous look.

Mom laughs. "Absolutely." She gives me her own look. "I've used up most of Monica's supply of Play-Doh during my time here."

"Play-Doh?" My mouth gapes open as I imagine my workaholic Mom playing with Play-Doh. "Why did you . . . do that?"

"To help me think." Mom shrugs. "I've realized that when I'm worried, it helps me to move my body. My fingers or feet or whatever. When I'm concentrating on something else, whether it's making a bowl with the Play-Doh or doodling on a pad of paper, it frees my mind to figure out the answer to my problem. It relaxes me, too."

"Huh." It makes sense. That's what softball does for me, after all. *Did* for me, before the pressure got so bad. It's what singing does, too. They take me out of myself. "I get it."

I don't realize I said the last words aloud until Monica smiles at me. "That's what we try to do here in therapy. Take you out of yourself so you aren't the same person who came in. That way, you can examine your worries and figure out why you have them and how you can react in a different way."

"That makes sense!" Dad's voice is jovial, like he's some jolly old man. "Should we be doing the same thing?"

Monica leans back in her chair, one of those swivelly kinds that I used to love to "take rides on" when I was little. "Well, that depends on how you cope," she says slowly. "What problems you're dealing with and what your normal reaction style is." She steeples her fingers under her chin. "That's why we're here, after all—to determine how you, as a family, can best communicate in the future. So that no one has to communicate with drinking or dishonesty or other maladaptive behaviors."

I stare at Mom with my eyes wide open. It's strange to hear someone call her out on her drinking. But I guess that's what they do in here. There's no getting away from it, after all.

Dishonesty? Is Monica looking at me? Do they know I'm hiding something? But I ask something else instead. "Maladaptive behaviors? What does that mean?"

Monica laughs. "Look at us with our therapy talk. Anna here has become quite fluent lately."

Mom rolls her eyes. "Unfortunately."

My eyes dart from Mom to Monica. What does she mean by that? Is it unfortunate that she's in therapy? That she had to stop drinking? Unfortunate that I'm a bad daughter who doesn't want to fulfill her mother's dream?

"It's unfortunate that I got so bad in the first place." Mom says, like she's read my mind. She places her hand on mine and even with all those different skin cells, it feels like it always does. Like when I was a kid and couldn't fall asleep without Mom's hand in mine. She was my security blanket.

Maybe we all need a security blanket at some point, when things are hard. Maybe alcohol was Mom's.

Monica starts out by explaining that this session will be our opportunity to talk about how Mom's drinking has affected us and what we need to do in the future. Then she turns to me and Dad and asks who would like to go first.

"Go for it, Veronica." Dad acts like he's doing me a big favor by letting me start. I wonder if he *is* trying to be generous. (Or if he's trying to avoid talking for as long as possible.)

Not that it matters. I can't back out now. Everyone's eyes are already on me. I feel like I'm on one of those reality shows Tabitha likes to watch, when some huge dramatic event happens and there's a close-up on one of the contestants talking about how awful one of the other girls is. How worried or concerned or angry she is.

There are no cameras in this room, though (I hope). No viewers or ratings to worry about. No scripts to follow, either. (Because as much as Tabitha insists that her shows are "totally real," I know that most reality stars are actually actors playing characters with scripted lines and manufactured situations.)

Those shows aren't real life. This is.

I haven't rehearsed, so all I can do is go off my heart.

"Why did you need alcohol?"

Mom's face crumples, but she takes a deep breath and grips onto the sides of her chair so hard that her knuckles turn white. "I was having a hard time," she says slowly. "Between making partner at work and just plain . . . life, I guess. I felt like I couldn't handle anything." Dad nods at Mom, and she gives him a soft smile. I wonder how much they've talked about all of this, or if it's news to him, too.

"Why didn't you ask for help?" I ask. "It's what you and Dad always tell me to do when I'm stressed out." *Not that I've listened lately.*

"I guess I—" Mom briefly meets Monica's eyes. "No, there's no guessing. The *reason* is that I didn't want to worry you two. I didn't want you to see me as weak. Or a bad role model."

"I'd never see you as weak—" Dad starts, at the same time that I jump in.

"Mom, you're a great role model."

Mom waves her hands around to encompass the entire room, then the grounds of Pine Knolls out the window. "A great role model? Anna the Alcoholic?" She snorts. "Hey, look at that. It even sounds good."

"Anna." Monica gives Mom a *look.* Apparently therapist looks and Mom looks are quite similar. I wonder if they give each other lessons.

Mom sighs. "I know, I know. I'm in here now. I'm an alcoholic. I can't change that and I never can."

Never is a really long time. "Does that mean you'll always be an alcoholic?" It's what they told us in school. It's what Dad talked to me about and what Libby and I fear.

It doesn't make sense, though. Shouldn't Mom *know* now that alcohol is bad for her? How could she still want it? It's like when I was a little kid and touched a hot iron. After the burn I got, I sure didn't want to do *that* ever again.

This whole experience hurts more than that burn ever did.

"I'll always be an alcoholic." A tear drips down Mom's cheek. "I don't want to be, but I know that ignoring it will only make things worse."

"What do you mean?"

Mom crosses her legs, then uncrosses them. She pulls her legs up on her chair and sits on them. She wiggles around like she has ants in her pants. "I could leave here and say that I'm better. After all, I haven't had a drink in thirty-five days."

Dad reaches out and gives her a hug. "That's amazing, Anna."

Mom smiles. "It is. It's been a struggle, but I'm at the point now where I don't *want* to drink anymore. I don't want my mind to be the way it was. I don't want to act the way I did."

I cross my arms. "Good. Because the way you acted stunk."

I expect Monica to say I'm being rude. Or for Mom and Dad to yell at me for disrespecting them. No one says anything, though, and Monica even nods for me to keep talking. This therapy thing isn't so bad.

"It did." Mom nods, and actually cracks a smile. "It totally stunk. I was rude and I lied and I was basically a mess."

"A total mess," I agree. *Am I lying now, too, though?*

Mom winces. "I deserve that. And I hate knowing that my daughter saw me that way. Like I said, I want you to admire me. Which is why I came in here, even though

I felt like I was deserting you." She wipes another tear away. "I still feel like that."

"I felt like that, too," I say softly. "For awhile. Well, sometimes I still do."

Another wince. I'm the total worst. I keep going, though. Honesty, right?

"And maybe that feeling of betrayal will never go away," Mom says slowly. "Just like for me, no matter how much time I spend in recovery and how many days I'm sober, there's always going to be a part of me that's vulnerable to wanting a drink."

"Always?" I ask.

"Always," Mom says. "But vulnerable doesn't mean that I will. Or that I want to. It just means I need to be careful."

Now Dad speaks up. "That's why your mom is going to be going to meetings, honey. Every day, in addition to the sessions with her therapist. She's going to keep on top of this so that if she ever gets tempted to drink, either because of work or something else, she has an outlet. Someone to talk to."

"But what about us?" I can't stop myself from asking. "Can't you talk to us?"

Mom smiles. "Oh, honey. I know I can always talk to you. I really do. But this isn't your responsibility. It's my problem to take care of."

"But what if I *want* to help? What if I *can* help?" I grip my hands together tightly. "I'm doing everything I can, I promise." A sob gets caught in my throat. "I'm trying, but it's so hard. I'm doing everything all wrong!"

"Oh, honey!" Mom reaches out and takes one of my hands, squeezing it gently. "You don't have to do anything. This is my responsibility, not yours."

"But I have to help you get better! I have to make life normal when you come home. I have to . . . I have to . . ." I bury my head in my hands, my tears and snot soaking my skirt.

"You have to what?" Mom and Dad ask at the same time.

I shake my head, misery covering me like a blanket.

"This is a safe space, Veronica," Monica says softly.

Is it? Is anywhere safe when alcoholism will be lurking around every corner for the rest of our lives?

"We want to hear what you have to say, honey." Mom squeezes my hand again.

"Absolutely." Dad looks confused, but his eyes are kind. I guess it must be weird to have to spend the whole month alone with me and suddenly realize that I have some big secret.

A secret that could ruin everything.

I guess I have to trust them, though. Trust Mom and Dad. Trust myself.

I take a deep breath and let it all out.

Thirty-Six

"I made the All-Star team." Mom and Dad start to say something, so I hold up a hand to stop them. I can't deal with another round of congratulations right now. "Wait. Let me finish."

"Let her finish," Monica adds. "This is her space now."

I nod at her gratefully. "I made the All-Star team," I say again. "But . . . I don't know if I want to play."

Mom's eyes are wide. What am I doing? I should stop talking.

I can't, though. My thoughts feel like a snowball rolling down a mountain, picking up more momentum by the second.

"I love playing. I really do." I look at Mom, begging with my eyes for her to believe me. "I'm proud that I was good enough to make the team. I just . . . don't love playing on that team. There's so much pressure and Coach Ortiz is always yelling and if I play, I'm going to be so busy and I . . . I . . . well, I really liked singing this year."

I feel like holding my hands over my eyes and peeking out like I'm watching a scary horror movie. My heart is pounding loud enough. I keep eye contact, though. I need to see how they really feel.

"You did seem to enjoy Chorus Club," Dad says slowly.

"I loved it!" I exclaim. Why isn't Mom saying anything? Did I mess everything up?

I talk faster to cover up my nervousness. "If I do the All-Star team I won't be able to keep doing Chorus Club. And I want to. My new friend Libby and I have been practicing for the talent show, and, yeah, at first we wanted to win so we could afford softball, but now I just want to win because it's been so much fun." I take a deep breath. Mom doesn't look mad. She looks confused, though, and twists around to look at Dad.

"Can't afford softball? Why can't we afford softball?"

Dad avoids Mom's eyes. "It's nothing you have to worry about, Anna. Really. I'm just being cautious."

"No, I want to know." Mom places her hands on each side of her, like she's bracing herself. "Is this why you don't want to play, Veronica? Because of some money issue?" She stares at Dad until he looks at her. "What money issue is this anyway? How could you make a decision like that without me?"

"Because I couldn't talk to you!" Dad raises his voice, then takes a deep breath before continuing. "You've been in here, leaving me to figure everything out on my own!"

Mom shrinks back into her seat as Monica finally

speaks up. (It took her long enough.) "Hold on a second. Let's all communicate calmly." She stares at each of us, one by one. She has a fierce therapist look, one that makes us all sit back and quiet down. "Veronica, let's hear from you first."

"Um." I feel like I'm in front of the class making a speech. "Dad said that it might be too much for me to do the All-Star team."

Mom raises her eyebrows. "And he made this decision based on what?"

She's doing that thing where it *seems* like she's asking me something, but she's *really* blaming Dad. It's an advanced Mom trick. Monica's on to her, though.

"Anna, if you have a question for Dan, please direct it to him."

Mom sighs and turns toward Dad. "Why *can't* Veronica play softball?" She sounds like she's speaking from a script. I hope Dad knows his next line, because I sure don't.

"I just thought that it wouldn't be the best idea for us," Dad says slowly. "Life will be busy now, Anna. Between your meetings and you maybe not going back to work and my jobs and me managing you—"

"Wait just a minute." Mom holds up a hand like she's a traffic cop waving a big red stop sign in Dad's face. "Jobs, plural? Managing me? Me not working? What's going on?"

"I got another job," Dad says quietly. "At the hardware store. I was thinking that you might not want to go back

240

to work, since you said that environment was part of what made you sick. This is my way of making your transition easier."

Mom's eyes soften, but her mouth is still a hard line. "Well, that's very nice of you, Dan, but you forgot to talk to me first."

"I'm just trying to take care of you, Annabelle."

Whoa. Dad broke out Mom's full name again. He must be really serious.

"By deciding things for me?" Mom's voice wavers. "I *am* still an adult, even if I'm in rehab."

I look at Monica, my eyes wide. I feel like I'm in church, eavesdropping on someone's confession. Should I even be here anymore?

Dad shuffles his feet against the carpet. *Shoofa shoofa shoof.* "I know that we'll be busy and I'm afraid of what will happen if we add an All-Star team schedule on top of everything else."

Mom sighs. "We can handle this, Dan."

"But what if you get stressed out and need me and I'm halfway across the state at one of Veronica's games?" Dad asks. It feels like we're in a big game of chess, always worrying about what the other player is going to do next as we move our pieces cautiously across the board.

"What if *I'm* there?" Mom counters. "I need to be able to handle myself. To not rely on you for everything. And we can't sacrifice Veronica through all of this. My alcoholism has affected her enough."

The three adults turn to me, like it's my move. I'm not sure what piece to use, though. They say they don't want to sacrifice me, but am I sacrificing myself? What do I *really* want to do?

"And yes, I *know* that I couldn't be reached," Mom adds after a second. "But you could have waited for me. You know I won't be in here forever."

Dad scoots his chair closer to Mom's. "I do know that." He sighs. "It just doesn't feel like it sometimes. We miss you, Anna."

"This month has lasted forever," I allow myself to say. "Not that it's your fault, Mom," I add quickly.

"Well, it is." Mom's eyes are sad, and her voice catches. "But I'm working to fix myself and figure out what I need. And right now, I *do* want to go back to work. I *do*," she emphasizes at Dad's concerned look. "I just . . ." She looks at Monica, who gives her an encouraging look. "I don't want to be partner after all."

Dad exhales, his chest visibly deflating. I can almost feel the released tension evaporate in the air. "Oh, thank God."

Mom snorts. She giggles. Dad does, too, and before I know it, they're both doubled over with laughter.

"Working those hours was a *lot*," Mom says when she finally catches her breath. "Along with the pressure to be a face of the company." She shakes her head. "I can't do that anymore. It doesn't allow me room for anything else. *That's* what I had to escape. That's why I turned to alcohol."

Monica raises her eyebrows.

"Okay, it's not the *only* reason," Mom says. "But it *was* a trigger. Something that made me want to drink. Something that I realized was getting in the way of my happiness."

Dad reaches out and gives Mom a hug. "I'm proud of you, Anna. You *are* a great role model."

Dad turns to me like he expects me to echo his words. And I want to. I *do* agree with him, after all. But Mom's words are still ringing in my head. *It doesn't allow me room for anything else.*

Does Mom feel the same way about work that I do about softball?

"Honey, you can still play if you want to. Really." Mom's smile is warm. It's the most relaxed I've seen her all day. In months, actually. I guess that's what honesty does. What recovery does, too. "You don't have to convince yourself that you'll find something better in singing. We can afford the team."

I can play.

A few weeks ago, those three words would have caused my heart to grow three times its size. Now, though, I'm numb.

I made the team.

I have permission to play on the team.

But do I want to? Would it allow me room for anything else?

"I don't want to play."

I expect Mom to fall on the floor. I expect Dad to faint. I expect our family to fall to pieces.

Everything has *already* fallen to pieces, though. The shards and pieces have been lying around me for months now. I've been stepping around the sharp edges so I don't cut myself. I've even had to put a few Band-Aids on.

Pieces can get put back together, though. Claudia's mom once told us about this Japanese technique of mending shattered pottery, where they fix the cracks with shimmering gold. That way, when something is broken, it's even better once it's fixed. The cracks are always still there, but the mending actually makes things stronger in the end.

More beautiful, too.

Maybe if I crack things some more, that strength will come to us.

"I don't want to play on the All-Star team, I mean." I look at Monica's rug when I say it, following the pink-and-yellow swirly pattern until the bright colors start to hurt my eyes. "It's a lot." I peek up at Mom and Dad, ready to bring my hands to my ears to block their yelling. They'll shout something about how I made a commitment to softball and it'd be irresponsible to break it. How they bought me new cleats just a few months ago and why didn't I make this decision before?

How I'm a big old quitting quitter who quits.

They don't say any of that, though.

Dad just smiles. "Sure."

Mom nods. "I'm okay with that."

Wait, what? I look back and forth between them, waiting for the anger to appear. For the early exclamation of "April Fool's!"

They're serious, though. They don't care.

"You're . . . fine if I just play rec league? And do Chorus Club, too?"

"Absolutely." Dad crosses and recrosses his legs casually, like this totally isn't a big deal.

"But . . ." I look at Mom. "Softball was our thing. You were a superstar. Won't it be weird for you if I don't play? Won't that hurt you? If you come back and things aren't how they used to be?"

"Oh. *Oh.*" Mom's eyes widen. "Hurt my recovery, you mean?"

I nod.

Mom brushes her bangs out of her eyes again. Maybe therapy is making all of us see more clearly. "Honestly, honey, I don't want things to be the way they used to be."

I tilt my head to the side. "But isn't that why you came in here? To fix things?"

"To fix things, yes. But not to send us back in time." Mom sighs, then gestures to herself. "Past Annabelle let her alcoholism take over her life. Past Annabelle couldn't deal with her emotions. I don't want to be that woman anymore."

"Oh," I say softly. Next to me, Dad's eyes shine brighter than they have in months.

"We don't need to bond over softball to be *us*. Not at all." Mom smiles. "I loved softball. I still *do* love it. But my time *playing* softball is over."

"Exactly!" I exclaim. "It's my time n—"

Mom holds a hand in the air. "Wait. I'm almost done."

I listen.

"I love playing softball with you. But not because you're good at it—which you are—but because you're my daughter, and I love spending time with you."

I smile. Mom smiles back.

"I love you being happy even more, though. And if softball doesn't make you happy anymore, then I want you to find what does. I want to bond with you in a *new* way."

I remember playing catch with Mom when I little. Last year, even. Softball was fun back then. No one was watching me, rating my skills, and telling me to give up the rest of my life. I threw, I caught, and I hit. I smiled, I laughed, and I ran.

It was all so simple.

"Softball does make me happy," I finally say. "But other things do, too."

"Then do those things. Love those things," Mom says firmly. "Because I love you."

"I love you, too, Mom."

"Life can be stressful, huh?" Mom asks softly.

I can barely get the words out behind the lump in my throat. "Maybe I should thrive off the pressure, or whatever. But I don't. Is that wrong?"

Mom stands up so that she looms over me, and gestures for me to stand, too. Then she wraps me in a hug so big it could encompass the entire world. "It's not wrong at all, honey. It's the same thing I've been realizing myself." Mom tilts my head up so I meet her eyes. "This world puts a lot of pressure on us—to be everything, to do everything, and to always be the best. I think sometimes we forget that we don't always *have* to be superstars."

"You don't have to be *anything*," Dad adds. "As long as you're Veronica."

"And you tell us the truth." Mom hugs me again.

"Just like we'll tell *you* the truth. And we'll trust each other." Dad gives Mom an apologetic look. "I'll trust you, too, Anna."

"Hey, Mom?" I pull back and look at her again. "I'm proud of you."

Mom's eyes sparkle with tears, and she doesn't even attempt to stop them from falling. Dad's crying, too, and wraps his arms around us both.

I can practically feel the gold hardening on the cracks around us.

Thirty-Seven

I thought that it'd be hard to leave Mom at the end of Family Day. I thought I'd cling to her like a little kid, begging her to come home with us and not leave me again.

And yeah, it *is* hard to say goodbye, to not know exactly when I'll see Mom next. But I know I'll see her soon, and that's almost as good.

After we say goodbye, after Dad and I hug and kiss Mom and promise that we'll always be here for her, after we drive home in a contented silence, the music playing softly in the background, after we pull in the driveway and troop inside, a bag of takeout food in each of our hands, the house doesn't feel so empty anymore.

It may not have Mom inside, but that's only temporary.

Like this softball decision.

I could decide that I don't like singing that much after

all. I could watch my friends play on the All-Star team and realize I made the wrong decision.

Maybe.

Maybe not.

All I know is that right now, *this* is the best decision. Like Mom not pursuing being a partner at her law firm. It's what works for both of us now.

And in the end, isn't "now" all that we have?

My phone buzzes as I'm settling on my bed to do some homework. Two texts, one from Claudia and one from Libby.

> Claudia: How'd it go???
> Libby: How's your mom?

I look at both their names. My best friend since forever and my new friend. The person who will always be there for me—if I let her—and the one who stepped up when I needed her. I know they'll like each other. I just have to make it happen.

I write back to Claudia:

> Can you meet me before the talent show tomorrow?

Then to Libby:

> Let's meet up early to rehearse one more time.

They both agree, and I lie back on my bed and smile. Then I turn on the radio and sing.

~~~~~~~~~~~~~~~~~~~~~~~~~~~~~~~

"Hey."

"Hey."

Libby and Claudia stare at each other, their eyes darting around like a bee trapped inside a mason jar. I know Claudia's not mad at *me* anymore, but what if she's mad at Libby? I imagine them yelling at each other like in one of those Disney Channel shows, where the girls screech and stomp around all dramatically. Will I have to step in to be the referee? Will I somehow get a bucket of paint thrown on me or we'll all fall into a big mud puddle while canned laughter plays in the background?

I shake my head and force myself back to reality, just in time to see Claudia give Libby a warm smile. "Thanks for being there for Veronica."

Tears prickle the corners of my eyes. Of course Claudia isn't screeching at Libby. I almost feel embarrassed that I expected them to fight over me—like sisters arguing over a favorite doll or something.

Claudia and Libby are better than that. It's why I'm friends with each of them. It's why they're friends with me. We're all nice people.

I'm starting to realize, though, that when it comes to friendship, "nice" has a lot of different meanings. Nice isn't just sharing your turkey sandwich with your friend when her mom packs her the dreaded egg salad. Nice isn't just saving someone a seat on the bus.

Nice is telling best friends about the serious stuff your family is going through.

Nice is more than actions. It's a state of mind, a willingness to let someone in. To know that they won't abandon you, no matter what you—or your parents—do. To know that you're okay just the way you are.

To know that you can make friends with your friends' friends, too.

"Of course I helped Veronica." Libby adjusts the shoulder of her top. We're wearing matching outfits for the show, which starts in an hour—bright pink shirts, jean shorts, and black ballet flats. Libby's mom added rhinestones to the shirts in this cool swirly pattern, which will hopefully catch the lights. We'll dazzle the crowd—in more ways than one. "She needed me and I was there."

"I would have been there, too—" Claudia starts to say, but I hold up a hand to stop her, then move out of the way of a few kids who've just arrived. We're waiting in the back of the town hall, just outside the door with the big PERFORMERS ONLY sign on it.

"I know you would have been there." The pit of guilt opens up in my stomach again. "And I should have told you." I want to tell Claudia that she *already* forgave me. That she shouldn't be—she *can't* be—mad at me anymore. Then I remember the way I feel about Mom. How maybe I *do* forgive her, but I may also still be a little bit (sometimes a lot bit) mad for awhile.

I let Claudia's comment go.

"I should have told you," I say again. "And I'm sorry."

"I know." Claudia shrugs. "It's okay."

"She told me for a reason." Libby's voice is hesitant, but grows surer with each word.

I look at her with a question in my eyes. *Are you sure you want to tell Claudia?* Libby nods back, then continues.

"My mom's an alcoholic, too," she says simply.

"Oh." Claudia's hand flies to her mouth. "I'm so sorry."

"No, it's okay." Libby shrugs. "It is what it is. And she's doing okay now. I mean, I sometimes worry, but there's no real evidence that I should worry."

I put my hand on Libby's shoulder. "I think we're always going to worry."

"Maybe. Maybe not." Libby bites her lip. "But right now, I do. A lot. That's why I understand what Veronica is going through."

Claudia crosses her arms over her chest. "I would have *tried* to understand—" She takes a deep breath. "I *am* trying to understand. And it sounds hard."

"It is." Libby and I say the words at the same time, then smile at each other.

"Anyway," I say. "I wanted you guys to meet. Because . . . well, because you're both my friends. And I think it'd be cool if we *all* became friends." I look at Claudia pleadingly. I know we used to think Libby was totally conceited, but now I know that she's changed. I want Claudia to see that, too.

Claudia smiles. "I can do that." She bites her lip. "I was really jealous of you two."

"And I was jealous of you!" Libby exclaims.

I speak up to break the tension. "Guys, you don't need to fight over me. I'm not *that* amazing a friend."

"Ehh, I guess not." Claudia's eyes sparkle.

"Hey!"

She reaches over and gives me a hug. "I'm just kidding." Then she turns to Libby. "Friends?" She sticks out her hand.

"Friends." Libby shakes it, a smile as bright as the sun spreading across her face.

Which immediately fades as Mrs. Pfeiffer, the lady who runs the talent show, sticks her head out the back door of the town hall. "Girls, are you part of the show? We need to start getting organized backstage."

Sparks of excitement burst to life in my chest. I jump up and down like we do during our softball warmups and start running through the lyrics of our song in my head. "Ready, Libby?"

Libby doesn't move, her sunshine now overshadowed by the darkest storm cloud I've ever seen. "Um. Yeah. Maybe. No."

Claudia peers at Libby's face more closely. "You don't look so good."

She's right. Libby's face is pale, almost greenish. She

looks more like Elphaba from *Wicked* than a future pop star. I take a step backward. "Are you going to barf?" Claudia hops back to join me at a safe distance.

"Maybe." Libby sinks to the ground. "I can't do this."

"Do what?" Even as I say the words, though, I know what she means.

"This." Libby waves her hand around, encompassing the town hall, then the other performers streaming past, all of them bubbling over with excitement. Like me.

Not like Libby.

"I thought I could and I wanted to support you and help you, but I feel like my chest is about to explode." Libby looks at the ground. "I guess I'm not a good friend after all."

"Of course you're a good friend!" My mind is spinning. I know that I can't *make* Libby do the talent show. That would be the meanest thing ever. Especially after how relieved *I* am that my parents aren't making me do the All-Star team.

I take a deep breath. "I guess I'll just have to do it alone." I twist around to look at the parking lot, which is starting to fill up with cars. A lot of cars. Each one with a lot of *people* inside it. My stomach begins to churn. I didn't think *I'd* be nervous, too. I try to make myself look all confident and turn back to Libby.

I may be a good singer, but I must not be much of an actor, because her eyes open wide. "Your face looks a little green," Libby says faintly.

My hands fly to my cheeks. "No. I'm okay. Really."

"You don't look okay," Claudia pipes up.

"I am! I promise." My voice wobbles, and Libby's eyes widen. I can almost see the struggle in her brain as she tries to get up, her legs shaking beneath her.

"I can do it with you." Libby closes her eyes. Her face looks *super* green. "Really. I'll be okay."

I can see how fast Libby's breathing, though, and if I put a hand over her heart, I bet it'd be beating double time. I shake my head and summon all my courage. After all, if I want to be a singer, I have to learn to perform by myself. "I won't make you do that." I nod firmly, more to convince myself than my friends. "I can perform on my own. The act won't be *as* awesome solo, and we probably won't win, but that's okay. I don't need the money after all."

"You don't?" Claudia and Libby ask at the same time.

"Oh. Right." My cheeks redden. "I decided not to do the All-Star team this year—"

"What?"

"Your parents won't let you?"

I shake my head. "No, it's not them. It's me. It's my decision. I'll explain more later, but I'm fine. Really. I promise."

They look doubtful, and I smile to reassure them.

"That means that I don't need the talent show prize money," I add. "So we don't need to wow the judges with our awesome moves for two." I try to sound confident and sure, but my words flop out like a limp spaghetti noodle.

"You were so excited about our act, though." Libby twists her hands together. "I ruined everything."

"No way!" I shake my head. "It's okay. Come on, let's go!" I force a smile, then start walking around the building to the front of town hall.

I turn back when I don't hear footsteps after me.

"No." Claudia shakes her head.

"Huh?"

"I mean, no. Or, yes, actually. Yes, you can still wow the judges." Claudia does jazz hands, then spins once, reaches for the sky, touches her toes and does a little shimmy. It's the exact move that finishes off my and Libby's dance routine.

My and *Claudia's* dance routine?

"I'll perform with you."

Thirty-Eight

I peek out from behind the curtains. The act before us, a mother-and-daughter cooking demonstration, is almost done, and I smile at the adorable toddler with brownie batter on her nose. The mom shows the audience their bowl full of batter, then whips a towel off the top of an already-baked pan of chocolate deliciousness.

"And this is what they look like baked!"

"They're super yummy!" The little girl grabs the microphone from her mom. Her mom looks at her expectantly, like she's cueing her next line. "Oh!" The girl's eyes widen. "And you can buy them after the show."

The audience claps and cheers as I close the curtain and move backstage. The auditorium is almost completely filled, but instead of making me nervous, like I'd anticipated a few minutes ago, the sight of all of those smiling faces out there excites me. *They're* not going to be rating how fast I run or how many balls I catch. (How many notes I hit, more likely.) Well, the judges may be, but the audience won't.

Winning the talent show doesn't matter to me anymore, anyway. What matters is having fun with my best friend and doing something I love. Enjoying life instead of competing for it.

"Are you ready?" I whisper to Claudia.

"Ready." Her eyes shine as bright as the rhinestones on our shirts. Libby's shirt is a little big on Claudia, so she tied it in this cool knot-thingie at her waist.

I squeeze her hand. "I'm glad we're doing this together."

"Me too." Claudia squeezes back. "And it's okay with me that you're not doing softball, you know. In case you're worried about that."

I nod. "A little bit, I guess. But I know we'll always find time to hang out, even if we're not on the field together."

"Absolutely. I'm going to do rec league again in the fall."

"Cool." So will I.

The mother-and-daughter act finally exit on the other side of the stage, and I peek into the audience again. I can just see Dad in the front row, next to Claudia's brother and parents.

"Oh!" I peek back at Claudia. "Your mom and dad are sitting together!"

Claudia smiles. "Yeah." She shrugs. "They don't fight as much now that they're living apart. We all even had dinner together last night. It was weird. I keep hoping that they'll get back together."

"Will they?" I try to see if her parents are holding hands or kissing or anything.

"Nah." Claudia shakes her head. "I asked and they said no. That it was sweet of me to hope, but that this is the way our life is now."

This is the way life is now.

Like Mom not being in the audience, no matter how many times I peek out to see if she's shown up. Because I know she's still in rehab. I know she won't be coming home for a few more weeks. But just because Mom's not here—just because Claudia's parents are getting a divorce—doesn't mean they love us any less.

"Up next is a song-and-dance act from Veronica Conway and . . . oh, it looks like we have a substitution." On stage, Mrs. Pfeiffer shuffles her notecards, almost dropping one. "I sure hope they're more coordinated than I am."

I roll my eyes. Adult jokes are the weirdest.

"Veronica Conway and Claudia Munichiello!" Mrs. Pfeiffer slides into the wings on the other side of the stage as applause fills the auditorium.

I look at Claudia as the music begins.

She nods, and we dance onto the stage.

~~~~~~~~~~~~~~~~~~

I check the time on my phone and try not to stare out the window again. Or tap my foot. Or stare around at the empty room. Dad had a meeting for his job (his one job—he quit working at the hardware store after Family Day), so he had to drop me off at the town hall early. Which is why I'm sitting alone on the stage, in a rickety old folding chair, right over the spot where Claudia and I did our talent show routine just a few days ago.

Tonight I'm not here to perform, though. I'm here for the support group that I finally agreed to go to. I'm still afraid to talk to everyone about my "problems," but Libby assured me that they'd all understand, just like she does.

"Here I am!" Libby rushes through the doors, and they slam behind her, echoing through the large room. During the talent show, this room was filled with people—people who all stood and cheered as Claudia and I sang the last note of our song in unison. My heart pounded as I stared out at the audience, my heart beating not with anxiety but with exhilaration.

There were a few babies crying, but there was no coach comparing me to my teammates or tallying up how many balls I caught. There was just applause. Applause *and* a shiny third place ribbon. (Claudia and I are going to share it, moving it from my room to Claudia's room every other week.)

It's not first place, but it's still something.

And I think I would have still been happy with no ribbon at all.

"It's okay." I get up from my seat and give Libby a hug. She's explained how the support group will work about a billion times already, but I still want to hear it again. "Are there going to be a lot of people here?"

"It depends on the week." Libby sits on the edge of the stage, her feet swinging back and forth, and I join her. She's a lot more comfortable up here when all eyes *aren't* on her. I feel the opposite, though. A big crowd is one thing—all the people kind of blur together underneath the spotlights—but a small group like this is something else entirely. Everyone will be able to see me, just like I can see them. I won't be able to blend in.

I won't be able to hide.

Then I remember what I've learned over the past month—that hiding has never solved anything. That honesty and openness are what got me here, to a place where I have awesome friends, a supportive dad, *and* a mom who will be coming home soon.

"Will they expect me to talk?" I swing my feet, too. *Bump bump bump* go my heels against the stage. "Do I have to tell everyone everything?" There *are* limits to honesty, after all. Especially with strangers.

"You can share whatever you want," Libby reassures me. "You *do* have to introduce yourself, though. So we don't end up calling you Mystery Woman Number One or something like that."

"Jane Smith," I suggest.

"Princess Marzipan of Sparkleville!"

I giggle as the door to the auditorium bangs open and two kids drift down the aisle. I look at them closely, weirdly afraid that I know them from school. They don't look familiar, though. And what would be the big deal if I *did* know them, anyway? They're here, just like I am.

"Everyone has problems," Libby says softly, as if she knows what I'm worried about. "But talking can help."

A few more kids straggle in. I think I recognize one girl from the lunchroom. She gives me a small smile, and I wiggle my fingers at her.

"Okay, kids, let's get this meeting started!" A tall woman wearing jeans and a tank top pulls a few more chairs into the circle, then waves her arms at us.

I start to look at Libby—for permission? Guidance?— then realize that I can't just follow her around all afternoon. If I want these people to help me, then I have to move into the circle myself. I have to ask for help.

Just like Mom did.

Just like we all have to do sometimes.

So I listen. When we go around to introduce ourselves, I tell the others about myself. About Mom and Dad and my friends and softball. About singing and school and how, finally, I'm maybe—just maybe—learning where I belong.

Acknowledgments

So many thanks go to my current and past agents, Kate Testerman and Brianne Johnson, who have both worked with me in different capacities to help this book enter into the world. Massive gratitude also goes to my editor, Kat Brzozowski, whose enthusiasm, kindness, and super-duper speed constantly reassured me that Veronica was understood, appreciated, and in such good hands.

A huge thank-you also to Jean Feiwel, Rachel Diebel, Melissa Zar, Kelsey Marrujo, Celeste Cass, Kathy Wielgosz, and the rest of the staff at Feiwel & Friends. I am forever grateful to be part of such a wonderful publishing house and imprint.

Cover designer Liz Dresner and cover artist Julie McLaughlin created the most gorgeous art I could imagine—I stared in awe when I first opened up my email and saw that starry sky. Thank you for bringing Veronica's world to life in such gorgeous lines and color.

Thanks to early readers of this book, including Pam Styles and Cory Eckert, who helped me with details about addiction, treatment centers, and alcoholism. Your honesty and guidance were essential to this process.

Thank you to my parents and in-laws, and to Jena DiPinto and Kate Averett, who are there for me every step of the way, every hour of the day. You are truly both best friends *and* sisters. To my friends, who prop me up when I feel self-doubt, make me laugh, and rail against the world with me—another thank-you goes to Sarah Linskey, Joan Powers, Heidi Carrington Heath, Monica Lundberg, Sarah Fink, Liz Clancy, Julie Clancy, Kelly Hager, Michelle Nadeau, Katrina Munichiello, Martha Crannell, and the Buttery Soft Librarians. You girls are the best part of the Internet.

Thank you to my writer friends, who understand how weird and wonderful this career is—Chris Baron, Rachel Simon, Katherine Applegate, Nicole Lesperance, Katherine Welsh, Chris Clark, Ali Standish, and all those I forgot here but still remember. To the teachers who have reached out and included me and shared my books—Nicole Mancini, Sandy Otto, Claire O'Neill, Allison Straker, Debbie Myers, Caitlin O'Connor, and Cassie Thomas, your students are so lucky.

I'm also sending a warm hug and all my love out to all the kids struggling with a parent who is dealing with alcoholism. You are brave and strong, and I am so proud of you.

To the ones dealing with addiction. Thank you for continuing to fight this battle.

To my family. There are no words to express how much I love and like and adore you all. Brian, you have never given up on me and make me feel special, talented, and enough every single day. Ellie and Lucy, being your mom is the best thing that I could ever be. I love you to the moon and back infinity times.

Last but never least, to my readers. To the kids, adults, librarians, and teachers who have read my books and told me how much my stories have touched their hearts. To the lovers of words who spread that love around. To the reluctant and the enthusiastic readers. Thank you all.